High praise to a powerful new author!

"Being a writer of traditional westerns, I couldn't imagine what the combination of vampires and cowboys could be like. Well, I just finished Colin Webster's book and now I know. Solid, never ending action with a twist at every corner. A refreshing change, I must say."

– Will Riley Hinton
Author of "Lonely are the Hunted" –

"Colin has done something that is very rare, and very special these days. He's written a good Western that you can sink your teeth into like a nice thick beef steak seared over the open flame of a camp fire. You can smell the desert sage and feel the grit carried by the wind and it makes you squint your eyes as you read. But this isn't your Dad's Western, some surprise elements are going to grab you. By the time you finish the book, you'll be wearing a cartridge loop belt to work. This is a great story and I am eagerly looking forward to the sequel.."

– George Hill
Author of "Uprising USA" and "Uprising UK"–

"*Blood and Tequila* doesn't just bend the mold of a traditional western, it shatters it. Great characters combine with a fast-paced plot to form a solid debut novel. And, c'mon. Cowboys and vampires--vampires and cowboys. This ain't your pappy's Saturday afternoon read!."

– Josh Clark
Author of "The McGurney Chronicles" and "Dakota Divided" –

"In Colin Webster's book, *Blood and Tequila*, the author has done something I didn't think was possible. Skillfully, he has managed to blend two conflicting genres, the Western and Sci-Fi. With Webster's strange but riveting mixure of cowboys and vampires, perhaps the book should have been called, The Quick and the Undead."

– RG Yoho
Author of "Death Comes to Redhawk" –

"Cowboys and vampires, what a combination, and Colin Webster does it with flair. *Blood and Tequila* is a rip-roaring read. This book is just plain fun."

– JK Jones
Author of "In Due Time" –

Acknowledgements

I would like to thank my mother and father for raising me with a plethora of western books and materials, and for filling my childhood with John Wayne and Louis L'amour.

I would like to thank my soul mate, Bryana, for always believing in me and supporting my long hours of writing and research.

My utmost gratitude goes to the Creator of heaven and earth, for putting up with my nonsense thus far, and not smiting me before I had the chance to finish this work.

COLIN WEBSTER

Blood and Tequila

Published by White Feather Press, LLC
www.whitefeatherpress.com

ISBN 978-1-61808-051-6
Printed in the United States of America

Cover design created by Ron Bell of AdVision Design Group (www.advisiondesigngroup.com)

White Feather Press

Reaffirming Faith in God, Family, and Country!

This book is dedicated to
my father, "Iron Mike" Webster,
who loved a good western.
I hope you're reading it somewhere now.

CHAPTER 1

Leaping onto a fast moving locomotive from horse-back isn't so easy as the newspaper accounts out east make it sound. Heck, just standing up on the horse is hard enough. During the last job, one of the gang lost his balance and fell off his horse before he could even think about jumping. We buried his share with him, which seemed like the thing to do at the time, and rode on. This time we'd give the newspaper's somethin' to write about, the biggest score the Clay Wilder gang had pulled off yet. I figured as long as they was gonna write about me, I might as well give 'em something worth printing.

We'd been waiting all morning for the train, and it still hadn't showed. Some of the boys had gotten nervous, and wondered if someone had gotten wind of what we was up to, others figured it was broke down at the station, and we'd be waiting a while.

Taking a train with only ten men was well within the realm of the possible, but this train was supposed to carry a military payroll, and that meant there could be guards. It bothered me that I didn't know how many there were, if any at all, but it couldn't be helped. Our best bet was to take the train hard and fast, too fast for anyone to react, and save ourselves the trouble and bloodshed of a drawn out gunfight.

The boys had just begun to argue amongst themselves when the train come chuggin' around the bend, they'd been causing such a fuss we hadn't heard it coming as early as we might have. A few of my fellow outlaws was caught with their pants down where they'd crept off into the brush to relieve nature's call. We couldn't wait, and we rushed for it.

We'd timed this one badly, and my horse was well ahead of the pack, racing for the train while it chuffed along, trying to pick up speed.

A scared-looking fella in the blue coveralls was shoveling coal into the engine like he was trying to win a contest, trying to make the big locomotive go even faster. I took offense to his haste, after all, we hadn't killed a single man yet, and didn't plan to. That was my rule.

I snapped the reins and felt the steeldust leap forward with even more speed. That horse could outrun the devil himself, I'd boasted as much a time or two. The rest of the gang was fading fast. A few gave up the attempt on the engine and cut right for the cars further back. They'd have a better chance of catching the train further to the rear, but I needed them up front where the army payroll bound for the Ringgold Barracks was sitting all wrapped up with a bow for yours truly.

The steeldust tore up the ground like the hounds of hell was after him, and I just kind of leaned over and grabbed a hold of the window on the side of the engine. No standing up for me, no'sir.

I'd almost let go of the horse when the engineer decided to give me a warm Texas welcome with the business end of the shovel.

A sharp clang rang out when steel met steel where my fingers had clung a moment before. I lurched back into the saddle and palmed my colt, snapping off a shot which screamed off into the big blue sky after ricocheting on the thick steel wall of the engine. I wasn't trying to put any holes in the engineer, but I did need him to back up some so I could get aboard. As the engineer retreated back inside the cab, I grabbed hold of the window again and flung myself up and over into the engine.

Just as I was getting to my feet I felt, rather than heard, the shovel blade whistling through the air and ducked just enough so it only crushed my hat and rattled my teeth some, rather than crushing my head like an eggshell.

As the engineer was coming around with the shovel again, I let go with a hard right and said a silent thank you to the good ol' Missouri, Kansas and Texas Railroad Company, Incorporated, for their policy of prohibiting engineers to go armed. It seems they didn't want to lose skilled engineers anymore than I wanted to have to kill them, so by my way of thinkin' we both made out like bandits, can't say the engineer, now crumpling to the floor of the cab, felt the same.

The two soldiers guarding the payroll must have woken up and got wise to what was going on, because they piled out of the door from the first car, rifles in hand. Just as their rifles was coming up, I cut them a grin and yanked the handle on the brake, stepping back as they tumbled forward.

The screeching was so loud I wouldn't have been able to speak over it, but fortunately a pair of colts pointed directly in your beater is an unmistakable, universal message. Them boys calmed down some, and about the time the train came to a full stop I'd had them both hog tied with a length of good strong rope.

That was about the time the rest of the gang came huffing and puffing up to the car and went to work on the strongbox. Some came over the cars and some were still riding, but I set back and rolled a smoke while they went to work on the box.

Way I figured it, I'd done the heavy lifting, and they could do the rest. Curly and Luke went back through the passenger cars to make sure the people kept calm, but we didn't take anything from them, folks were a lot less likely to risk their hides for some government notes when their own was safe and sound. Besides, there was enough in the strongbox to make sure we'd live out the rest of our days rich men; or more likely, the way we spent it, have a few months jubilee down south of the border and then start a ranch or other enterprise somewhere far, far away from Texas. The Idaho Territory was nice this time of year, or so I heard.

When the box opened, Ike Turner gave a long, low

whistle.

"Shucks, would'ya look at that!"

The box wasn't full of bank notes, it was solid gold bricks. They gleamed bright under the hot sun, and a similar gleam could be seen in the eyes of the assembled bandits looking on. I eased the leather thong back on my other colt, real slow-like. There was something about the sight of a pile of gold that did queer things to a man's mind, maybe even persuade him to abandon the sacred bonds of thievery and think about taking it all for his'self. I was content with my share, but it was as if you could see the wheels turning in some of the other feller's noggins.

"Nobody move!"

"Reach for the sky fellers!"

As one, the eight of us looked up slow and careful-like to see Curly and Luke on top of the strongbox car. They were holding their rifles on us. Some of the gang raised their hands; I just kept building my smoke.

We'd picked up Curly and Luke a few months back, they were brothers who'd run afoul of the law out Missouri way and hightailed it out to wilder country to seek their fortunes anew. We'd only had a handful of small scores in that time, I'd no doubt they must've been planning on a betrayal at the first opportunity worth the risk. Then there was the chance they'd been Pinkertons all along, though I'd watched Curly carve a fella up in a knife fight in Santa Fe something fierce, and that wasn't the kind of thing those Pinkerton agents did.

I did the only thing a man can do when someone's got the drop on you with a long rifle; I gave them my best grin. "Whiskey Jack" Watson was trying to catch my eye, he had his back to the pair and I could tell he would make a move at the first opportunity. The rest looked alternately frustrated or scared, but Jack was cool as a bubbling brook up in the mountains and deadlier'n a rattler in your bedroll.

Here I was, a fortune almost in my hands, enough to end

my days of wickedness and robbery, and two cornshuck-
ers were going to either take it away or cut me down in my
prime. It's from such moments that legends are made, or
at least that was my way of thinkin' back then. I didn't yet
know if they would write about this in the papers or on my
headstone, but I was determined to have my say in the matter.

I began to speak, low and easy. The first thing to do when
a critter's pulling a gun on you is to get him to calm down
some, and these boys were mighty keyed up, jerking their
rifles this way and that, trying to cover all of us at once.

"Now boys," I said, and the rifles swung back on me,
"There's more than enough for us to all leave here rich men.
If you're not happy with your share, let's have a chin wag
about it, but there's no cause to pull guns on your brothers in
crime..."

"The box is ours Clay. You all jus' step back a pace, and
we'll take it and be on our way. If'n y'all behave, might be
we'll drop a brick or two and not bother pickin' it up."

I didn't cotton to that plan myself, but those twin barrels
pointed at my belt buckle were a mighty convincing companion to their argument, so I took an easy step back. Then
another. I wanted them to think they'd get their way.

"Alright boys, if that's the way you want it. Must say
though, I take it kinda' hard, seein' how we been riding the
trails together. Thought we was partners..."

"Ain't no such thing as partners in this business Clay, you
know that!" Luke yelled from top of the car, "You'd do the
same to us!"

"Would I Luke? What do you think boys? Have I ever
cheated a man out of his share? I've made the lot of you a
passel of money, and have I ever failed to split it even-like
with each of you?"

Billy Joe Blanks muttered something about a certain card
game up in Fort Worth, but the rest nodded and grunted
something to the effect that my statement was, in fact, true.

And it was. Despite the fact that I'd planned and scouted all of our little ventures, and took the lion's share of the danger, I'd made an even split all round. I figured a lack of jealousy among our little band of thieves was worth more than the small extra percentage I might've commanded. Perhaps I was wrong, since one man always strives to outdo the other.

I licked the paper and finished the smoke, trying to look calmer than I felt, since Luke's trigger finger looked a'mighty shaky. The distance from my hands to my Colts seemed a mile away.

"Now fellas, have you thought about just how you were going to move this much gold? We was gonna' split the notes among our saddlebags, remember? As it is, among the dozen of us we're gonna' have the devil's own time packin' it outta here. How you think you two're gonna' move it all by yourselves?"

Curly and Luke took a split second to share a glance, and I could see they hadn't quite thought that far yet. If the score had been a pile of bank notes like we thought, they might've at least taken most of it, but there was no way to move this much gold in their saddlebags.

I almost made a move right then, but before I could work up to it, the big black holes of their muzzles stared back at me like a set of cavernous eyes. My mouth was dry, but I had a powerful urge to swallow.

Curly shouted, "Billy Joe, drop your gunbelt! The rest of you back up! Billy Joe, you go grab the horses, empty the saddlebags, and bring them here. You fellers'll load them up with gold for us, and we'll use 'em as packhorses."

Those words sealed their doom. There was a slight pos-sibility they'd make it out of this before, but now every man here'd shoot it out rather than be left afoot in this country, especially since the army would be out in just hours, just as soon as the train failed to appear with the payroll. Billy Joe had dropped his gunbelt as ordered, so that was one more man out of the fight. That meant four against two, with them having the drop on us, and more significantly, their rifles were both pointed at me.

I'd watched a magic show at a small one horse town in east Texas once. They were a traveling theatre troupe on the way out to the big cow town's where folks had a lot of money to spend, and not too many places to spend it. Most folks there were amazed, but it didn't take me a second to figure out it was all misdirection. He'd call folks attention to a wand or a bright copper coin, and in his other hand he'd be making something disappear into his robes or fooling around with a hidden lever or pull string. It seemed the trick was to make a body center his attention on something else, and make your move. It was time to make me some magic.

I cocked my head to one side as if listening for something.

"Y'all hear that?" I asked, and let my eyes go wide.

Everyone glanced around, even Luke, though Curly wasn't buying it. He just kept staring at me over the sights of his rifle with those cold, beady little eyes.

"Sounds like hoof beats! I'd swear there's no way the army could've got word this fast though. You think it could be a posse?"

Curly shifted his eyes up to the horizon, just for a moment, and that's when I flicked the cigarette into the air, stepped to the side, and drew.

The world erupted in flying lead and thick puffs of smoke. I palmed both Colts and began snapping off shots. Curly jerked and his rifle went off, kicking up a spat of rock and dust just a hair to my left. He levered the rifle and shot again; I felt something tug at my sleeve, but my next shot caught him in the ribs. Luke's rifle spat flame as fast as he could lever the action, cutting down Rip Carlson and Bob Henry in their tracks. Billy Joe was scrambling to hitch up his gun belt again so he could draw, the fool, and "Tough Tom" Billings of Montana fame took two slugs to the chest before he rolled over in the dust, deader'n a doornail.

My fifth shot caught Curly in the gut and he staggered back, dropping the rifle. Curly was mortally wounded, but desperate and wild-eyed, he drew his guns and set to. My sixth and seventh shots struck home, but Curly didn't seem to feel them, so I took careful aim and sent the last right above his left eye, and Curly went back to whatever hell had birthed him. Dust to dust.

Before I had Luke in my sights he took John Robbins down with a slug to the neck, John was kicking in the dust and making a gurgling sound I don't even want to think about. Whiskey Jack shot Luke through the heart, and Luke stumbled, hanging in the air for a long second before tumbling off the roof of the car onto the rocks below. Jack turned him over with the toe of his boot, and Luke stared up through a mask of blood, began mouthing something, it all came out in a rush of syllables. Whiskey Jack calmly thumbed back the hammer of his gun and sent it home. I think that was the first shot I actually heard.

The gunsmoke was thick and acrid and my ears were ringing something fierce, but work needed done. Billy Joe was muttering over and over about how he'd tried to get a shot off, Jack told him to shut up and plug his wound. Both Whisky Jack and John Henry Tarville had taken slugs, Henry had one in his thigh and Jack had one through his chest. He was wheezing a bit and coughing up a little blood, but he swore and cussed so much while Billy Joe stuffed a clean kerchief in the wound soaked in whiskey that I thought he'd make the ride.

The rest of us leapt into action. We put John Henry and Jack on the roof of the first car with rifles, so as to discourage the curious while the rest of us loaded the loot. As chance would have it, we were now able to load Curly and Luke's horses down with their weight in gold, plus some, as well as fill our own saddlebags full. As we were stuffing the bags, I kept a watch on the rest of my gang, but everyone was pretty well focused on getting our ill-gotten gains onto

our horses and then, well out of range of the army or whoever else might come to seek justice for our crimes.

I had a bullet burn on my left forearm, but other than that
I was none the worse for wear. A quick dose of whiskey, one
splashed on my arm, the other on the back of my windpipe,
did for that, and having bound up the wounded as best we
could, we set off south with saddlebags full of gold.

Whiskey Jack was laughing as we rode, taking long pulls
of his ever present bottle, till it ran down his beard and onto
his bloodstained shirt. I kept quiet for the most part, but
couldn't wipe the grin off my face. I had in my saddlebags
more money than I'd dreamed of, and all the years to spend
it stretched out in front of me. But even for all that, somewhere deep down in the pit of my stomach, there was an
unaccountable sense of dread growing like a ball of ice.

I did what I always do, and kept my grin on, riding for the
Rio Grande while the big red sun cast long shadows as it set.

CHAPTER 2

B illy Joe Blanks slapped another hundred on the table, and went back to fondling the Mexican girl in his lap. I slapped down a stack of bills to match his, as the girl blinked twice to let me know he only had a low pair. I was holding three aces, and keeping my cards close. I didn't cotton to the bar girls or their profession, or to having them help liberate me of my money, though I wasn't above using their services to teach Billy Joe a lesson in gambling.

At the end of the lesson my fee would only be hundreds, and I reasoned it was cheaper than the thousands he'd lose over the years if he didn't learn he was just no good when it came to wagering at cards. I'd been teaching him this lesson for the last three nights.

I took a long pull of a bottle of indeterminate liquor I was told was whiskey, and thought of rattlesnake poison. It couldn't be, as rattlesnake poison probably tasted much better, and would be more agreeable to my stomach.

The village was called Rio de Sangre, and its tequila was served hot and its women hotter. It was a den of sin and lawlessness, the kind of place a desperado could hole up and hide out until justice forgot. We put Whiskey Jack and John Henry Tarville up in a hotel, and sent them plenty of provisions. Jack had a fever for a few days, and every time he had a coughing fit there would be blood, but he just made a careless jest about it and called for more whiskey. He joked that if he died, at least it would be as a rich man.

After a while Billy Joe threw down his cards and went upstairs while the dark-eyed beauty went off in search of other prey, after I slipped her a cut of the winnings. We were taking turns guarding our saddles and their contents in the stables, and I went by to make sure Tanner Jackson and Hank Struthers were at their posts. They were sharing a bottle, but only looked half lit so I wandered on down the road a piece, building a smoke as I went.

Bam! I got hit like a ton of bricks by the prettiest pair of dark eyes coming around the corner. Those same eyes went wide as she saw the big gringo lug standing there gaping open-mouthed like a sack of potatoes wearing a gunbelt in the middle of the road. My Spanish ain't so good, but I knew enough to tip my hat and say "Buenos Noches, senorita," and give her a charming smile. I knew it, but somewhere along the lines my tongue and my hands got the signals all mixed up and I swear I tipped my tongue and spoke out of my hat. At least that's what it must have looked like.

She gave me a small, shy smile for my trouble, and swayed as she carried the bushel around me, giving kind of a curtsy as she walked by.

I turned as she went past, and I swear the devil himself taught women how to sway their hips like that, and she must've been the star pupil. After she turned the corner I realized my mouth was still hanging open, so I did what any reasonable man would do in that situation and shut it and went tearing after her. I rounded the corner skidding on the heels of my boots, straight into a large and rather solidly built padre' in the middle of the street.

This time, I tipped my hat properly, having full use of my faculties, and managed, "Buenos noches Padre', er, donde esta la senorita?"

My accent was terrible, but I gather he got the picture, because he advanced on me the way you'd shoo off a mongrel, and was talking up a storm, I think I caught something along the lines of "Hombre Malos", and "Vamonos", and I'm sure the rest wasn't very complimentary.

The villagers may have been more than hospitable to our money and tolerant of our wild ways, but I also knew there weren't too many better ways to get in trouble in the border towns than to offend or mistreat the local Padre. The peasants were a peaceful sort, and often put up with quite a bit of mischief at the hands of wandering banditios, and we were, but there were stories of those desperados who carried things too far, and met an early end to their wicked ways.

I muttered my apologies, and turned to go on my way. As soon as I was around the corner, I tore off around through the alleyway in the other direction, but it was too late. The dark angel was gone. I was sweating and dizzy and all discombobulated. I'd never had anything like that happen to me before. Maybe it was the bad liquor, or maybe the Mexican sun was just too hot for my blood, but I was feeling something churning in the pit of my stomach like a team of wild horses was trying to kick their way out. Enough.

I doffed my hat and plunged my head into the nearest trough, and came up shaking the water off like a dog. Two of the little kids across the street were pointing and laughing at me. I made like I was serious, my hands hovering over my gun butts. They looked scared for a second, but when I gave them a grin they went along with the game, two of them making pistols out of their hands. I brought my own finger-gun up slowly, until one of the urchins cocked his thumb and let it strike home, then I put my hand over my heart and staggered, then fell backwards into the dust.

The kids erupted in laughter, and gathered their "hero" up onto their shoulders and paraded around. I looked up to see one dark eye staring at me from around the corner of an adobe building down the street. Long lashes batted a few times and the eye was gone.

Great. I hauled my carcass up off the dusty street and walked fast to the alleyway where last I'd seen my quarry. Nothing. I pulled my hat down onto my ears hard, turned on a heel and strode off. I'd no need of games. What I did need was a good strong drink.

Minutes later I was cozeyed up to a bottle of dark amber

liquid in the back corner of what they called a saloon here. There were a few other locals inside, some of whom were well dressed, and a pair of gringos who kept to themselves in the opposite corner. They didn't worry me much, as there were plenty of folks who dipped down into this part of Mexico for one reason or another, usually not too different from what brought me and my friends to this charming little village. This wasn't our first rodeo, and my gang knew better than to flash too much cash around or talk about the treasure in our saddlebags up the street.

I was on my fourth shot, trying to wash the vision of a petite girl with dark eyes out of my mind, when a shadow fell on my table.

"Pardon me friend, thought you could use some company."

I looked up to see a tall man, maybe six foot five, with a few days growth of beard and a sweat stained shirt giving me a toothy smile.

He didn't wait for permission to sit down, but hooked a chair with one long leg and then kind of collapsed back into it. His hands stayed near his guns.

"You'll have to excuse the intrusion friend," he said, even though I didn't, and he'd called me friend again, even though I wasn't, both of which tended to add up to trouble.

"See, me and my pardner over there," he nodded towards the man who remained seated at the other end of the saloon, with a sour expression on his face and a tied down gun on either leg, "See, we was just wonderin' something."

"Oh?" I said, mock interest on my face, but I'd already made up my mind how this conversation was going to end. I'd no idea what their game was, but it was all window dressing at this point.

"See," he leaned in, "me and my pardner, we jus' couldn't help but notice that you looked, well, kind of familiar. In fact, my pardner is of the opinion that he know's you from somewhere's, that mebbe somewheres he saw a poster with

13

your likeness on it."

And there's the rub. Either these two were bounty hunters, and brand new at that, because any bounty hunter worth his salt would have just dry gulched me and be half way back to the territory by now; or these two wanted to extract some sort of hush money for me, which didn't make them too bright, because who in their right mind tries to bull money out of some desperado in a Mex border town, unless they're either desperate or stupid?

The heels on their boots were run down something fierce, so maybe it was the latter, although the tall man's confident manner left me to gather they thought they had me pretty well boxed in and pinned down, so maybe it was both.

"In fact," The tall, toothy one said in a whisper, "he thinks you might just be none other than Clay Wilder."

One of the well dressed Mexicans at a nearby table stood up suddenly, plunked down a coin, and walked straight out of the saloon. I eased back in my chair. I was young and I suppose still a little brash then, because some small part of me was pleased to be recognized, even if I found what would come to be distasteful.

At that moment, Tanner Jackson and Hank Struthers strolled in, which meant the watch had changed. That was a good thing, because not only were there two of my compadres here to back me up if things went south, but there'd be two fresh men guarding the treasure, in case this wasn't about me at all. Most anyone who rode the hoot owl trail would rather target an admittedly lightly guarded cache of gold than go up against the famed badman, Clay Wilder. I smirked, because I was covered either way. On the one hand, because other than a few bricks at the top of each saddlebag, the lion's share was buried in the corner of the stable, on the other, because I was, indeed, Clay Wilder.

The two men didn't seem to notice my brothers in crime entering the saloon, other than a cursory glance, which seemed to rule out bounty hunters. Anyone tracking me would know my gang rode with me, these fools had likely just seen a wanted poster somewhere, and thought they could extort a quick payoff from a wandering desperado and be on their way.

Maybe they weren't a bad sort after all, it seemed a shame to kill them.

Now that I had them sorted out, I didn't see much point in waiting.

"Now, friend," The tall man gave that toothy grin again, "Maybe you is Clay Wilder, and then again, maybe you isn't. But either way, a couple of fellas could probably be persuaded to-"

His sentence was abruptly cut short as I kicked his chair out from under him. His long limbs tangled as he went down, and I palmed my Colts, pointing one at the sour looking stranger in the corner and another at the ball of limbs on the floor. The sour looking man hadn't even reached for his gun, and his eyes were wide.

The man on the floor threw his hands up.

"I didn't mean nothin' by it, friend! I was just-" I was sick of his slick and greasy talk, so I struck out with the heel of my boot and laid him out cold. I didn't like what I saw in the sour man's eyes.

"No need for gunplay, "Friend". You just drop that belt, real easy like with your left hand."

The sour man froze, and then his eyes got hard. A scared man is an unpredictable man, my Pappy used to tell me. You never knew what someone would do if they got frightened enough. If I had wanted to kill him, I would have done it already, but that never dawned on him, and before I could say anything his eyes went hard and he made his play.

Time slowed down as I watched the hammer slam home and the gun bucked, sending a 200 grain slug right between the hombre's ribs. He slammed back against his chair, sitting down, hard. His eyes went blank right there. He was dead. You never could tell. Some men soaked up bullets like lemonade, and kept coming, others seemed to give up the ghost as soon as they heard the gunshot, figuring it was all over but the visit to the pearly gates. Good luck with that one fella.

Tanner and Hank took the still-unconscious man outside, tied him to his horse, and slapped it on the rump to send it on its way back towards the territory. I stepped out back and built a smoke. I had briefly entertained the notion that now that I was a rich man, I'd never have to kill again. But for a man with my reputation, that would never be true. There would always be some young rooster wanting to make his reputation, or some lowlife wanting a cut of what I'd right-fully stolen, or a lawman seeking justice for my crimes against my fellow man.

I needed a new name. I would shed the one I now carried like a lowdown snake sheds his skin, and head off some-where with tall mountain peaks and cool streams, and make a new name for myself. I could claim to be a miner who'd struck it rich in Alaska, or out California way. Folks out west respected a man's privacy, and I wouldn't be the first to leave one past behind and start a new, more honest life.

I was thirty three. Same as the Preacher men said the good Lord was when he began a'preachin' the gospel. Maybe that meant something. Maybe it didn't.

"You killed a man tonight."

I just about leapt out of my skin, and probably would have drawn and fired out into the darkness, like a greenhorn who hears a catamount call in the middle of the woods on a dark night. But the voice was so soothing, that I knew it had to be her.

"I did." My voice was flat. It felt like an admission of guilt, although by my own code I never would have felt like I was in the wrong, even as distasteful as I found the event. It still felt liked I'd been tried and convicted by a jury, my own conscience, for some terrible crime. It was the way I'd imagine Adam admitting to Eve what he'd done, like there was nothing that he could keep from the woman he... wait a minute, that was the other way around or something. Maybe if'n I'd paid more attention in Sunday School I would have turned out different.

"He tried to kill you, but you killed him instead."

"Yes."

I struck a match and lit the smoke, more to see her face than anything else. In the dull red glow she looked stunning, eyes wide but absent reproach, utterly unhorrified by the killer in front of her.

"What's your name?" I asked softly.

"You should leave this place." She said, and melted back into the darkness.

I wanted to reach out for her, but didn't. I wanted to ask why, but didn't. I just captured that face in my memory, forever, out there in the darkness.

Tanner and Hank were buying rounds at the bar, and I joined them.

Two men from the kitchen carted the body off, I dropped a fistful of dollars in one of their hands, and made it understood in my halting Spanish that the man should have a proper burial.

In the wee hours of the night, when Billy Joe and John Henry were on watch in the stable, the rest of us gathered round a table in the shadows, tossing back liquor and sharing our plans for the future. I kept my own to myself, but was more than happy to listen to the others plans for the rest of their lives.

Will Green and Ike Turner, who were cousins of a sort, were going west to open up a saloon on waterfront in San Francisco. Billy Joe said he'd join them, but he was going to buy a ship and sail around the world, having adventures. We all had a good guffaw over that.

Hank Struthers was going to build a cabin up in Colorado somewheres, and spend his time hunting and fishing. Tanner Jackson declared he would go back east, and distribute a large portion of his wealth getting his extended family of sharecroppers out of debt. John Henry Tarville said he didn't know what he would do, except a lot of the Parisian whores out Louisiana way were going to become very rich women.

I never had no truck with houses of ill repute. My mother might've paled at the idea of me turning out as I did, but there were some lessons she taught me that I never abandoned. Someday, somewhere, I'd find me a gal to settle down with. Now that I was done with my days of lawlessness, perhaps I just might find her somewhere. She'd be waitin' for me on some dusty prairie, and I'd just know it was her the moment I laid eyes on her. She'd never need to know the kind of man I'd been, and we'd start a new life, together, and raise kids what knew better than to follow the kind of life I'd led. Hogwash, I knew, but a man has to have his dreams.

Suddenly, out of the blue, a wild eyed man came tearing into the bar.

Hombres! You must leave! There are...soldatos outside, they have guns! They mean to take you! They are-"

A shot rang out in the sudden quiet, and the man arched backwards, vainly trying to catch hold of the doorframe as they fell out into the street. They'd caught up to us, and if there was any doubt, that the soldiers, they had guns, that put the lie to it, right there.

We hit the deck as the night exploded with gunfire, slugs crashing through the windows and the open doors.

"The army came for us! But we're south of the border!" Billy Joe yelled in disbelief.

"You didn't think they'd just let us keep it did you?" I hollered back over the gunfire, popping up long enough to send a pair of slugs out the closest window. I didn't want anyone getting too brave out there until I had a chance to figure out a plan.

"Wait a minute! Who's on watch with the horses?"

"Whiskey Jack told us he'd be able to watch them all by

his'self, and for us to come in and have a drink! Said he was feeling a'mighty better!"

I cursed myself. Even after a long day's drinking I should have had the sense to realize we had too many men in the bar. Was this betrayal? I had a hard time believing ol' Whiskey would turn on us, even with the saying about honor among thieves and all. It was awful strange though, him sending the others away, though I couldn't think of how he could've called the army in, the town didn't even have a telegraph office. More importantly, why would he turn the rest of us in, he could've just as easily ridden off with his share of the loot, the rest of us just settin' here drinking like a bunch of fools and all. He was rich enough as it was, and Whiskey didn't seem like the greedy type, at least for a career train robber. Ok, I guess thats not saying anything a'tall. I resolved to ask him at the first opportunity.

First things first, escape. I reached for a bottle lying on the floor, it still had some whiskey in it. One of the .45-70 slugs careened off something and smashed the bottle to bits, just before I grabbed it.

Leaping to my feet, I ran for the bar and dived over, a hail of bullets smashing the bottles lined up on the wall above me. It's a shame to waste good liquor, but then again the liquor in Rio De Sangre took second place to rattlesnake piss, so I guess it was no real loss.

The rest of the boys were returning fire as best they could, while I grabbed two of the bottles, and stuffed two alcohol soaked rags in the necks. I let a bottle fly towards the entrance, where it broke and engulfed that half of the structure in a spout of flame. I'd have to rely on the back entrance not being covered, which would be pretty stupid indeed, but that was the best chance we had. Hopefully the soldiers had been interrupted getting into place when the man rushed in to warn us, otherwise we'd get cut in half on our way out, I was relying on blind chance that the soldiers would have been eager or foolish enough not to cover the back. Stranger things have happened.

"Follow me boys!" I shouted, and we rushed out the back door, firing into the night. I hurled the second bottle, where it broke and lit up the night in flames as high as a man. To think I'd been drinking that stuff.

In the light of the flames, I saw we'd walked into a death trap. I must've been born under a cursed star, because the building around the saloon created a kind of funnel, boxing us into a nice channel so we had no choice but to rush the soldiers lined up at the end of the long alley or die where we stood.

If this was to be my last hurrah, I was determined to go out with a bang. Palming both Colts, I snapped shots with one after the other, and the rest of the boys did the same. John got near torn in half by a hail of slugs, and I think he took one for me too, when he staggered across my path. Will green was cut down a second later, and next thing I knew I was dragged by the others back inside the burning saloon.

"There's too many, Clay! What do we do?!" Billy Joe screamed in my face. I thought he really needed a shave, and a good bath. Its funny the things you notice at times like that.

I might as well just kept on noticing things, since there wasn't a durned thing we could do about our predicament. I'd like to say I had a brilliant plan in mind, but prayer was pretty much the next thing on the list, and I didn't think the good Lord was of a mind to help such rascals as we.

"Hey! Estupido! Aqui!"

Even over the din of the gunfire, I'd recognize that voice anywhere.

She was in a third doorway, a section of the wall opened outward. A series of steps led down behind her.

I couldn't help but smile as I saw her. Her eyes locked with mine, and there was a moment when time slowed to a stop. She looked at me, and...a stray bullet screamed across the room and shattered one of the lamps next to my head.

Moment over.

I kept my head down and sprinted across the hail of gunfire coming through the door and windows to the hidden door where my senorita stood waiting. She looked irritated, even more so when I picked her up and flung her over my shoulder like a sack of potatoes. One of the boys pulled the section of the wall shut and we were in darkness.

CHAPTER 3

The soldiers cursed and offered opinions as to just how we escaped. We listened there for a moment in the darkness, and I gathered their commanders name was Major Willhelm, who from the way he ordered his men about, sounded like a real horses hind end.

"You there, enlisted man, bring me that bottle! I always have a drink after a good battle!"

I heard the sound of a bottle being upended, and then a crash as it was dashed to the floor. It sounded like the good major was being sick all over his boots. Welcome to Rio De Sangre, Major, enjoy the tequila.

I set the kind and gentle senorita down, since she was pounding my back with her fists, and it was making a heck of a racket. Striking a match and shielding it with my hand, I took a quick count of who all I had with me. Billy Joe, Tanner, Hank and Ike were here, along with one a'mighty angry Mex gal, and yours truly. I could only wonder at what became of Whiskey Jack, but that old coot knew how to handle himself, and he was probably hunkered down some-wheres, if'n he wasn't laughing his head off leading a trail of gold-laden pack horses out of town.

The senorita was mumbling something under her breath, I remember distinctly hearing the word, "cabeza", but that was it. It was probably better that way, given that it didn't sound very complimentary.

"You," she pointed at me, "You bring trouble to my vil-lage, now men are dead, even a good man who tried to warn you!"

"It warn't us that shot 'im!" Billy Joe protested, "It was

them thar soldiers that dunnit!"

She slapped him across the face, quick as a snake, whap whap, one on each side. Fiesty.

"Quiet! Follow me, you silly men! This passage goes down quite a while. Here, hold that match still so I can light this torch."

I could see her face more clearly in the torchlight, and man she was a sight to behold. She was downright breathtaking in the sunlight, by the flickering light of the torch, even more so. I felt like an idiot, mooning over a gal so, but some things a feller just can't help.

"Hey, whats with the secret passageway? Seems like we're in one of them dime store novels or somethin'!" Snorted Ike, just before Hank smacked him one upside the head.

"What kind of books you readin' dummy? What kind of idiot writer tells stories about little secret passageways in little Mex border towns?"

I had to admit, it seemed pretty farfetched, but here we were.

"Bastante! Quiet! You'll bring the soldiers down on us! Now, try not to fall behind, and keep your mouths shut!"

I followed the petite form down the steps. Her dress was bright white, else I wouldn't have been able to see much of her, even in the torchlight, it was near pitch black.

After minutes of picking our way down the winding stairs, the passageway leveled out, and took on a more gradual downward slope. The darkness seemed to get thicker here, as if it threatened to swallow up the flame itself. We found two more in the walls, and lit them. It helped, just a little.

I put my hand on the gal's shoulder to make her stop.

"Just where are you taking us? What is this place?"

"This town has been here a long time, and is no stranger to secrets. But only a few know of this passage, and others. We will come out on the edge of the canyon; there will be horses waiting for you there."

The hair on the back of my neck stood up. I was willing to take on faith that this gal meant to help us, but it seemed as if there must have been others involved, if they were setting aside horses for our escape. We'd dropped a passel of cold hard cash here, but I didn't think for a minute that bought us the loyalty and kindness of the local citizenry, so there had to be another angle.

"Why help us?"

She sounded angry when she replied, "Do you find it so hard to believe that we are no friends of the American army? It is not the first time they have crossed our borders, nor, I think, will it be the last. That man, their leader, is well known in towns on this side of the border. Any enemies of those soldiers are friends of ours. By the way, what did you do to them to make them hate you so? Surely you are not just common banditos, no? Ayayai, my Uncle's saloon is utterly destroyed!"

I doffed my hat and bowed with a flourish.

"Uncommon criminals, no ma'am, we're criminals of exceptional refinement and taste. Those soldiers outside, we stole their pay. I suppose they aim to get it back."

She cocked her head and glared at me, as if deciding if I was making fun of her. If I'd ever had a touch with women, perhaps I was losing it. All in all, it wasn't that far of a stretch to believe the locals had plenty of ill feeling towards the army. There was no love lost on our side, over the Alamo, though something about the way this girl wrinkled her nose when she got mad kept me from relating that sentiment.

The tunnel finally opened up into a large sort of hall.

There were openings all throughout the hallway, and I could imagine a network of tunnels all winding and twisting underneath the town. It was truly mind boggling, I had no idea how long it would take to dig all these tunnels in the solid rock. The flickering torchlight showed some kind of carvings in the walls. We must be getting closer to the canyon by now, we'd twisted and turned some, but the cliff beyond the village was much less than a mile away, and I'd guess we'd been walking for the better part of an hour. I'd tried to keep my bearings, but it was near impossible in this underground labyrinth.

The senorita pulled and tugged for a moment at a heavy wooden door with an iron handle. Just as I was about to step in to help her, it creaked open with a loud, long, groan. The other fellas were running their hands along the walls examining the carvings, but I was more interested in our hostess.

She turned back to me suddenly with a strange, sad look on her face.

"You never told me your name." Her voice was soft, like silk.

"Clay. Clay Wilder." I said, with a goofy grin. She wanted to know my name! Sheesh. I was hopeless. Better to die in the gunfight upstairs, than fall head over heels for a woman. At least you kept your dignity intact.

"What's your handle, senorita?"

She looked up and met my eyes.

"Maria Sophia Marta De La Villanueva," she spat out quickly. Try saying that three times fast. I couldn't. Maria.

"Clay?" She said softly, looking at the ground.

"Yes Maria?" I answered hopefully.

"Lo siento. I am sorry," She muttered quickly, and slammed the door shut behind her. We were locked in.

CHAPTER 4

W hat the hell'd she do that fur?!" Ike shouted, as I drew my guns and put my back to the wall. This place was all mystery, and none to my liking. When someone locks a body in someplace, there's usually a reason, and it ain't never good for the fella what's been locked up.

While the rest of them stood muttering curses and wondering just what was happening, a shadow zipped through the room, causing the torches to gutter and the flickering light to whither to embers.

When the flames sputtered back to life, Tanner lay sprawled on the floor, his throat torn clean out. All hell broke loose. The torchlight gleamed briefly, something moved in the corner, and everyone started shooting. Something whooshed through the room again, and I ducked on instinct, felt the air rush above me. I snapped off a shot, but it was too late.

One of the torches went out. We needed light! Another sharp whistle cut the air as whatever it was whipped through the room again, from one passage to another, and Hank went spinning in circles to collide with the wall, spraying blood and firing his revolver into the floor. Another torch went out. We were down to one.

I yanked the torch away from Billy Joe and tore Tanner's jacket off. He was past caring. We were getting cut to pieces as it was. If the light went out, we were all dead men. I knew that was true as gospel. I lit the jacket all at once, tossed it in the center of the room, and did the same with Hank's shirt and vest. We had a bit more light. This time I heard the whooshing sound coming down one of the passageways, and shouted "Down!" just in time.

We dropped like so many stones, and whatever this thing was, its momentum carried it right through the room and into yet another of the rough hewn doorways carved into the rock.

We yanked everything we could off the dead men and set it aflame, tossing the burning clothes to various corners of the room.

I closed my eyes and listened hard for the sound of approaching death. It was coming down the passage just behind me. I stepped into the opening, thumbed back the hammers of my Colts, and cut loose. In the flashes of flame I saw something terrible, all teeth and claws, and I spun out of the way as it sliced through the room again, this time with an awful scream. I hoped to God I'd hurt it badly, but the whooshing sound came again. This time from two different places.

"Take your jackets off and light them on fire!"

"Clay? What-"

"Just do it!" I bellowed, and we shrugged out of our jackets just as fast as we could and balled them up in the flame.

I motioned for Billy Joe and Ike to get to each side of one of the doors, and as I stood by another, I told them in signs what I wanted them to do.

Just as the whooshing sound that preceded the creature's arrival grew louder, I turned around the corner and slung the burning jacket out so it unfurled in the stone archway.

There was a sudden screech and then a smacking sound and cinder flew everywhere, in my eyes and up my nostrils, until I was coughing and spluttering, ducking away from the door to get away from the growing flames. I couldn't see anything, but the heat was intense.

Stinging tears washed away the debris, and as soon as I opened my eyes I wished I hadn't.

Something writhed and capered in the middle of the room, twisting around with an inhuman shriek as the flames engulfed it.

I stood motionless, frozen, staring at something that just could not be.

The jaws distended impossibly wide, the fangs long and jagged, hideous to behold. Bone white skin blackened and charred before my very eyes, the screaming was loud and pitched so high I wanted to cover my ears.

Instead I fired. I gave the one in front of me both guns, and Ike and Billy Joe did the same to their creature, only theirs was only half on fire, throwing itself against the stone wall hard enough to crumble sections of it, trying to put out the flames.

The creature stopped writhing in pain long enough to throw its arms back and scream defiance at me. I shrunk back from the heat, and it seemed to just fall apart in a pile of smoldering ash.

My guns empty, I yanked out the derringer from my waistband and kept firing at the retreating, half burnt creature Ike and Billy were doggedly weighing down with lead. The creature was dragging its shoulder against the wall to extinguish the last of the flames, and with one last snarl at us, it sunk back into the shadows from whence it came. Ike put a few shots down that passageway by way of goodbye, and we immediately set to reloading in the flickering light.

In a few seconds we heard echoes coming down the long dark tunnels, and the sounds were something I hope never to hear again in my life. I can't even describe them, except to say that my blood curdled in my veins and more'n a few hairs turned white that very moment.

We'd just killed something from the very depths of hell, I was certain, and now there were a bunch more of them out there. And they were angry.

I thumbed shells into my Colts in time with my heartbeat, which is saying something.

I'd just been shut up in the dark with some kind of unholy terrors, and instead of being scared out of my wits, I was just downright mad.

The echoed howls died down, and I imagined wave upon wave of monsters descending on us.

Fortunately, discretion is the better part of valor, and we turned back to race up the steps toward the cantina. Better to face a whole regiment of soldiery than whatever was down here.

The only problem with the plan was that the passageway was gone. The wall was solid where it shouldn't have been, though I'd never heard it close. We pried and poked at the rocks around where the door should be, and I ran my fingers over the rough stone but could find no cracks or telltale flaws in the rock.

Before us was stone, behind us almost certain death. My pappy was a good old rebel though, and passed on to me the wisdom he'd gained surviving the great war between the states. One of the truths he'd passed on was that the best way out of an ambush was straight through. It was the only thing the enemy didn't plan for, folks didn't plan traps so's you could escape them by fleeing.

I would have given much for a few sticks of dynamite right then, but my wishes were worth whatever the two corpses that used to be Tanner and Hank had staining their britches. The smell was awful.

Arched stone doorways ran all around the room save the far wall where we'd come in. Nothing indicated where they went, but I was pretty sure there must be another way out of here. Might as well pick any of them.

I set one of the revolvers down and spun it. Luck, be a lady tonight.

The barrel came to rest pointing at one of the doors. Good as any.

We each kept a hand on the other's back, I took the lead with both guns ready, each of the other two men held a torch in one hand and a gun in the other. The light only shone a few feet ahead of us, like the blackness was a hungry thing, eating up the light and growing stronger and stronger.

The air grew dank and foul, the further in we went. Now and again we came upon carvings roughly hewn into the walls. The crude etchings showed men with enormous jaws filled with long jagged teeth, smaller figures knelt with arms and faces lifted towards heaven. It gave me the creeps just to look at it.

I had the feeling something was watching us closely, just out of reach of the light. I hoped whatever was down here, by burning one of them we'd have taught them some respect, and I wouldn't have to repeat the trick.

The floor of the passage began to slope upwards, which we took to be a good sign. We came to a fork in the tunnel. One led upward, and one led downwards.

We took the one that went upwards. We walked for what seemed like hours. The tunnel stretched onwards, carved through the ground long ago. The place was like a tomb, and no doubt it was for many a soul. It might even serve as mine.

Just as I was shuddering at the thought, the sound of rushing water filled our ears. It seemed to come from the walls themselves. At nearly the same time, we heard a sound that can only be described as in between a cackle and a growl, and it was coming this way. I stuck out a hand, trying to find a recession in the wall to press back into if something came a'whooshing up the tunnel. The wall was wet, weeping water in tiny little droplets. A river! I'd heard that sometimes, deep in the rock, there were rivers running through the earth, surfacing now and again, but traveling great lengths all through the land. An underground river wasn't the kind of thing you wanted to take a ride on, and it was a testament to the dire straits we were in when my heart leapt with sudden hope. Another growled laugh, this time closer, and behind us.

"Billy Joe, get on the other side of me, and hold the torch high. Back to back you two!" I barked the order, and began running my hands over the wall, looking for the wettest spot.

I'm not the biggest man, but I'm broad shouldered and when I take hold of something, it generally moves.

I felt out the likeliest spot and rammed my shoulder into it, again and again. Kicking out with all the strength I had in my legs, I willed that wall to break. When the growl came again, even closer, I began throwing myself at the wall like it owed me money from a poker game, and felt something give a little. There was a long low sound like something coming up the tunnel from both directions, awful fast.

"Whatever you're doin' Clay, you'd best finish it, because it sounds like our number's done been called. It's time for the big dance!" Ike helpfully pointed out, his voice cracking.

Backing up to the opposite wall, I flung myself at the wet rock in front of me.

"Nah Ike, It's just like Santa Fe, remember? With the bank and the dynamite and the vermillion-painted lady?"

Ike wailed a piteous cross between a laugh and a moan.

"We'll make it through this too!" I yelled over the whooshing air and water.

The sudden rush of water caught even me by surprise. An entire section of the wall collapsed, and the black water covered us.

I'd heard a time or two about the outhouses folks were building inside their homes at places out east. It sounded disgusting, but it was the thing to have, to hear the eastern fellas tell it. They said you pulled a chain and a feller's leavings were washed down a hole with a rush of water. I imagined this was what it felt like to be flushed down one.

My skull bounced rudely off the rock walls a few times, as I was swept end-over-end away with the current. It made me dizzy, both the tumbling and the bouncing part, but I managed to hold my breath. At least one of the other fellers were still with me, I knew, because now and again I'd feel a hand clutching at my boot or take one of their boots to the face as they kicked and struggled hopelessly against the current.

They say nothing is stronger than running water. I knew that was a load of manure, because I'd seen a tornado in action a time or two, but I'd have gladly taken my chances for some air at that point. Heck, I woulda' killed for some air at that point.

In some small part of my brain I found it interesting that even though all was pitch black inside the underground river, I could still see colored spots swimming before my eyes. Just as well to drown as to be slaughtered by some creature though.

A flash of light. Was I finally going unconscious? Then another. My head broke surface, and I reflexively gulped for breath. The river had come up into a section where there was a hole in the rock far above, and I managed to turn myself around just in time to see a rocky overhang, heading my way fast. I gulped a breath and tucked my head back under water just in time. The river dropped straight down, and pulled me down with it. I couldn't see Billy or Ike. As the light faded back away the last glimpse was of a pale form tearing up water swimming toward me. One of the creatures!

It was a good thing I'd replaced my weapons in their holsters before breaking through the wall. Tugging a Colt free as the current knocked me head over heels in the underwater tunnel, I took a guess and fired at what should have been behind me. A tiny flash of light was quickly extinguished but in that second I saw jagged rows of teeth stretched wide mere feet away. The creature was coming for me.

I thumbed back the hammer again, just as a pair of unbelievably strong hands took me by the shirt. Stuffing the barrel up between us until it hit something hard, I pulled the trigger and was rewarded with a short, sharp burbling squeal. I struck out with my left fist at the sound and couldn't be sure if I'd hit the rock or the thing, so just shoved back and kept slipping the hammer back and jerking the trigger. More squeals, but the hands didn't let go.

And then there was light.

Light, and a bright blue sky as I was suddenly in open air, and falling fast. The pale form seemed to hang in the air for a second above me, glaring malevolently, looking so hideous I forgot about the fact that I was suddenly falling.

The figure above me burst into spectacular flame, so bright my eyes squeezed shut, and the smell of burning sulfur filled my nostrils.

As spectacular and unbelievable as the sight above me was, I was quickly and inevitably drawn back to the fact that I was falling.

I craned my head around to see the ground was a long way down.

I tumbled. My hands and feet struggled against air, helplessly seeking purchase where they would find none. The ground rushed up to meet me.

CHAPTER 5

The buzzards circled lazily in the sky. The faintest wisps of clouds stretched out like big white feathers behind them. The sun was like a burning ball of fire in the sky, and thats what one feller from out east had told me it was, so I guess that was fitting.

After a time, I wiggled my toes, saw the tips of my boots move. So far, so good. I lifted a leg which hurt like the blazes. Another good thing. It was mere minutes before I lurched to my feet, coated in wet sticky sand. Lightning bolts shot through my skull, but that meant I was alive, or in a special sort of hell that looked just like Mexico. Come to think of it, nah, never mind. I was too beat up for a snappy remark.

The wash was full of piled sand, the odd piece of broken pottery, and pools of stagnant water. I took a long drink from one, before retching it back up again. The world spun on me, and I set back down for a while. I pulled out the makings of a smoke, but the pouch was wet, and the papers all stuck together. I took stock of what else I had. One gun was still in my holster, I only had to crawl a short way to find the other. It took a while to rinse the sand out of it, and thumb out the empties.

I'd done for what, three of the critters? It was somewhere around noon, judging by the sun, and I had a ways to go to get shut of this town before nightfall. It didn't take a Harvard man to figure out those things must've been mighty averse to sunlight, as the last one had shown a marked allergy to it.

I was safe in the light, I reasoned, but after that all bets were off. Putting one foot in front of the other, I set off in search for a way up out of the canyon. The walls stretched out far on either side of me, so I dug out a coin and tossed for it. Heads. I went east.

Another half hour of plodding through the muck led me to dry ground. A little path, the kind only a goat could follow, wound up into a crack in the rock. I took it.

The climbing was hard, and in my condition it was harder. In some places the path was so narrow I had to suck in my stomach and blow the air out of my lungs and kind of cram through.

I was scratched up with thorns and briars, and covered in rock dust, dried mud and sand by the time I reached the top, but I threw an arm over a ledge and grinned. I felt I'd earned a drink for my troubles.

Visions of bellying up to the bar and whetting my whistle were cut short as I remembered the soldiers. And Maria. They were both still in town, no doubt, and I'd a score to settle with each.

The brush leading out from the village was thick and high, so I was able to pick my way close to the town without too much trouble. Halfway there, my progress was arrested by a strange sound. Someone was hollering to beat the band, and the voice was familiar. It only took a second to locate the hole in the rock, leading down to blackness so dark I could barcly make out the figure below.

"Jee-hosephat! How'd you get up there Clay?!"

"Never mind that you fool! Shut your yap or you'll bring the soldiers down on us!"

It was Billy Joe, clinging to a broken off branch wedged between the rock walls of the underground river. He must've been clingin' there a spell, 'cause he was shivering and pale as a sheet. All in all though, I think he had a better time of it than I did.

"Ya' gotta' git me outta' this here hole Clay! I'm F-f-f-f-freezing my tail off!"

"Simmer down Billy, we all know yer mother cut it off when you was born! Now, just hold on a while longer, and you might just clean the stench off yer hide! I'll be back!"

"Wait! What the.. .Clay!"

The town was close, and I could see a shed out back of one of the houses on the edge. Hopefully there'd be a length of rope inside, and no soldiers on patrol. Catfooting it around the edge of the structure, I slipped the rusty lock with my pocketknife and eased inside.

Waiting a while for my eyes to adjust to the light, I found the length of rope I needed, and in a rare fit of decency, plunked down a handful of coins on the table. Perhaps there's something about almost meeting one's maker that leads one to be a mite more mindful of one's actions. In the little things at least. If there was a scale, mine was awfully listing to one side. It'd take a sight more than a few coins to balance that scale. I chuckled to myself.

A sudden footstep at the door, and before I knew it I was staring over the sights of my Colt at a smallish man, clad in the dress of a local peasant. He froze. I raised a finger to my lips, slowly. He mimicked my action, then quick as a flash tore off around the corner.

Moving fast, I ran back to where Billy Joe was still a'callin' after me.

"Clay! Thank the good Lord! I thought you'd done gone and left me!" "I will at that, if'n you don't grab this here rope!" I dropped it down to him.

"Tie it off around that scrawny box of kitchen matches you call a chest, and I'll haul you up." Billy was tall, but one of the lankiest devils I'd ever had the misfortune to run across. The tunnel was just wide enough to accommodate his passage through some spots. There are advantages to bein' able to take a bath in a shotgun barrel.

It was a good thing, too, since I had to haul his carcass up some seventy five feet, give or take.

He'd just reached the top, soaked and scraggly as a newborn kitten, singing the praises, when a shot rang out. That little peasant had done gone off and called the soldiers. I regretted payin' for the rope, and heck with the scales.

Me and Billy Joe took off into the brush, hunkered down behind a twisted hunk of mesquite. It was the best cover around, and I was wary of ricochets. The soldiers began a pattern of searching fire, which is a way of sayin' they shot the living hell out of the thicket we was in.

After a moment they left off, and my wheels started turning, figuring out what to do next. We were backed up to the cliff, hidden for now among the thorns and brambles, but it wouldn't be long till they came in after us, and no matter how many we accounted for, I was willing to bet it wouldn't be enough. There was no way out of the thicket but through town or off the cliff, and I'd already done that trick.

A whiff of smoke caught me by the nostrils, and Billy's eyes went wide.

"They mean to burn us out!" He said in a frightened whisper.

"Then we best not be about when the fire gets here," was my only reply, and I set off stalking through the brush. The smoke grew so thick you could cut it with a knife and sew yourself a pair of socks out of it, and I tied my still-wet bandana across my face to keep from coughing. We crawled like injuns, low and quiet, all the way up to the edge of the brush. Soldiers in blue uniforms shifted back and forth at the edge of the thicket expectantly, straining to see through the thick clouds of smoke. I passed one end of the rope to Billy Joe and explained what we were to do. He looked at me with wide eyes, but swallowed and nodded.

"Now!" I screamed, and with a rebel yell we leapt forth out of the smoke and brush, the rope stretched taught between us. With Billy on one side and me on the other, the three soldiers we could see were caught in a moment of frozen surprise, and then went down hard as the rope caught them across their chests. We didn't stop to see what happened next, but took off up an alley as a scattering of shots went screaming off the adobe buildings behind us.

Racing up one alley and down the next was like running through a maze, and from the confused shouts behind us it didn't seem the soldiers were having any more luck. With any fortune, most of the soldatos would have been surrounding the thicket, leaving us the main street, and more importantly, the stables, free and clear to make our escape.

We rounded a corner to see two privates turn quickly towards us, and as they raised their rifles I bulled forward and slammed bodily into them. One went down hard, bouncing his skull off the hard wall, and as the second one scrambled back to his feet, Billy Joe kicked him in the face in passing, leaving him sprawled in the dust.

We reached the backdoor to the stables without further incident, which I thought was surprising; only a fool would leave our horses unguarded. As we entered I saw the reason for the major's apparent lack of care regarding our means of escape.

The horses were gone. All of them. Billy Joe began tugging me back out the door, but I shook him off and took a moment to check the floorboards above our hastily buried treasure. Gone.

My heart sank, not just from the loss of the treasure but from what could only mean the betrayal of an old and trusted friend. Me and Whiskey Jack had ridden the hoot owl trail for years upon years, and if I had been so foolish as to trust any of my little band of cutthroats and thieves, I had to admit it was him. Curse my eyes.

It stung worse than the bullet burn I'd picked up somewhere in the last few minutes, now weeping blood through the side of my shirt.

Just the same, I was glad for a sign he'd made it out alive, and that meant he and the treasure were somewhere else, and that somewhere was somewhere I planned to be, and the sooner the better.

The soldiers were hollering and bellowing orders and shooting up everything in sight, coming up the road toward the stables. I guess it didn't take a genius to figure out the first place we'd go. Billy started to duck out the other door, then jumped back in like a scalded cat, and whispered that there were more coming the other way.

For the first time I noticed that the stables also served as the repository for all the dynamite and gunpowder in the town. The paint on the barrels and boxes was dull, and I probably would have noticed it before had I not been so giddy at the thought of my saddlebags, full of gold. It was a mistake I doubted I'd get to make twice.

We were trapped like two rats in a tin bucket full of firecrackers.

Soldiers covered both entrances. I set my teeth, ready to ventilate the first man through the door. After that, it was a safe bet the whole host would open fire, and if we were lucky, we wouldn't feel a thing when the shots inevitably struck the explosives piled high around the stalls.

"You in the stables!" The stuffy Major's voice sounded like he was on the stage at a theatre, playing the role of conquering hero.

"Throw down your guns, and come out with your hands held high!"

He gave a low, throaty chuckle.

"You'll be given full benefit of the justice system of the U.S. Army, before we hang you!"

The soldiers outside thought that was a real riot.

"Throw down my guns! Like hell! Why I'd-"

"Psst!"

I turned, sharply, to see the big padre gesturing from a hidden door in the wall. Not again! "No time! Vamonos! Rapido!"

The priest turned and ran off down the passage.

This all seemed like that French thing, deja vu, 'ceptin it was happening all over again. Still, my options outside weren't looking none too bright, and you can always trust a priest, right?

I tugged Billy along with me, and stepped warily through the door.

CHAPTER 6

"Hold it right there Padre," I growled, setting the barrel of my Colt against the back of his head. I reckon' the good Lord would take it kind of hard, but I wasn't trusting no one at this point.

The priest turned, face grim, hands lifted away from his sides.

He'd led us through a passageway into the sanctuary of the old Spanish mission at the end of the long main street that ran like a scar through Rio de Sangre.

"You'd better have a passel of answers baled up behind them teeth, and you'd better start shuckin' them pronto, comprende?"

The priest nodded.

"You and your...companion may want to have a seat, this could take some time."

By quickly thumbing back the hammer I indicated that I preferred to stand, thank you very much, and that he'd better get on with it. Or something to that effect.

The priest nodded in acquiescence to my eloquent statement.

"Senor, you must understand, there are forces at work here far beyond anything you have known. I am Miguel Santos Cortez, and I am...pleased to make your acquaintance. You seem to have become familiar with the creatures that infest the bowels of the city, which may make what I am about to tell you somewhat more believable. My story begins many years ago, though since we do seem to be a bit short on time, I shall try not to burden you with details. I was born in this village long ago, the son of the priest who preceded me.

This was all kept a secret of course, and I was merely known as the bastard boy some wandering vaquero left in my mothers belly. She was very young, and madly in love with my father, willing to bear the shame of this lie in order to protect him. They were not allowed to marry, of course, and my family, such as it was, lived in squalor and neglect.

I was given odd jobs to do, my mother was an outcast, abandoned by her family, and it fell to me at an early age to earn our daily bread. I fed horses, mucked out stalls, and before long I had taught myself the rudiments of the smith's trade, so I could-" He wiped his face with his hand suddenly. "This is all unimportant. In my free time I would wander the caves and caverns in the countryside, searching for and sometimes finding pieces of pottery and other trinkets. Once I found a great rusty espada, a sword, wrapped in a tattered cloth next to a pile of bones. These and other such finds I would bring to the priest at the mission, at the time I did not know he was my father.

He was always kind to me, and would give me a few coins for my 'treasures' and sometimes he even had a piece of candy for me. I always brought the coins home to my mother, and the candy to my little sister. The good priest always was delighted with my finds, though I saw none of them displayed around his small home next to the church. At the time I merely thought him a kind man with a rare taste for things of the distant past. Some of the pottery I would find was grotesque, primitive representations of hideous creatures our pagan ancestors worshipped in these lands before the Spanish brought the light of Christ to our world, centuries ago.

The one admonition the kindly priest always gave me, other than to make sure to say my prayers and always be kind to my mother, was to never, ever, go near an old mission, long since abandoned, nearly hidden in an arroyo at the edge of the canyon. In my boyish curiosity, it was a recipe for disaster. Mystery, ancient things, and the sense of the forbidden. How could I not go? Senor, I tell you, it remains to this day my greatest regret. The sin I would commit would echo through the years, leading to the loss of countless souls-again, senor, forgive me, I don't mean to prattle.

I rushed through my chores the next day, everyone must have wondered why the little bastard boy was shoveling el estiercol...ah, horse manure, with a smile on his face bigger than the canyon. In my head I saw myself discovering a great treasure, and riding back into town on a great white horse, triumphant, able to see my mother and my sister never wanted for anything again.

Even though I attacked my chores like a madman, it was late in the day before I was allowed to leave my employer and go home for supper. I never went home. Instead, I gathered the items I had stashed in my satchel, and I ran the miles to the old mission, dreams of gold and redemption glittering in my little eyes.

I arrived at dusk, but since I had brought a lantern and matches, I was not worried. It would be pitch black inside the ruins anyway, and I was not given to fears of what might be creeping in the darkness. That was long ago, when I knew no better.

The mission had been abandoned for at least a hundred years, and there was nothing but the odd piece of broken pottery or bits of rusted metal inside. I searched for what seemed like hours, but found no sign of gold or valuables. My little heart sank. I sat on the remains of the altar and wept, crying out to God for some way to save my family from the crushing burden of our poverty. In the depths of my despair, I collapsed back against a section of the floor, and it gave way under me. I fell. The next thing I remember, I opened my eyes, a sharp pain throbbing through my skull. By some miracle, my lantern had landed next to me, unbroken. I closed my eyes and gave thanks to God, that he had left me at least this light to comfort me as I died. At the moment I had no doubt I would. The ceiling was some twenty feet above me, and I had told no one of my plans, or where I would go. No one would come for me. I was alone, in the dark, trapped. I was finally afraid.

After a time of self reproach and despondency, I resolved to pick myself up and explore my final resting place. By the light of the lantern, the great cavern revealed its contents. There was no way in or out that I could find, but the contents of that place were beyond anything I had ever dreamed of. The walls were carved with reliefs similar to the hideous art I had found inscribed on pottery in the surrounding caves. Carefully wrought golden statues and bars were piled high around the room. Goblets and platters of gold were strewn about the floor, as if hastily thrown in and forgotten. Great golden crucifixes were crudely affixed to the walls and even the ceiling. But the most terrifying discovery lay silent in the middle of the room. A mouldering corpse lay in re-pose atop a great stone bier, a gleaming golden spike stuck through his chest. I could not help but approach, transfixed with terror and wonder both. The carefully wrought crucifix atop the spike glittered golden in the candlelight. It was a work of art of such terrible beauty I immediately knew it was the most valuable piece in the entire treasury that would be my tomb. A grim smile stretched across my young face. God had answered my prayer. I was indeed, a rich man. And I would die one. The dead man before me had no doubt been killed in a struggle over this very treasure, my mind played out a great battle in which the chief treasure had been finally seized from his hand and then used to murder him. But try as I might I could not fathom what would lead men to abandon a treasure such as this and build a holy place atop the room to hide its contents forevermore.

I was torn between the respect for the dead I had been taught and the gruesome appearance of the murdered man, the weapon still in his chest. It was a gruesome scene. The thought of lying eternally beside such a sight chilled me more than my own impending doom. It seemed suddenly quite reasonable that my grave-mate be made more present-able, and after all, wouldn't covering him properly be a much more respectable act than leaving him be? In truth, something about the great golden spike glittered behind my eyes, and I wanted it dearly, to have and to hold for all eternity.

I took hold of the spike with both hands and braced my feet on either side of the corpse's great barrel chest. The sudden disturbance caused the jaw to drop open, and a puff of dust to rise from its open mouth. I leapt back, screaming. I had imagined the dead rising, coming for me in revenge for my attempt to take his "treasure" from him. When nothing happened, I began to laugh at myself, and my silly superstitions. The dead could not rise. With renewed courage, I stood over the corpse, grasped the spike, and pulled. I was strong for my years from all the hard work I had done, but still it took all I had to tear the spike free. It had been driven through the body all the way into the stone itself.

The spike came loose with a sudden crumbling of stone, and I fell back onto my rear with a thud. The spike clattered to the floor, echoing ominously throughout the hall. At the same time a sudden draft swept through the cavern, though there seemed to be no source for it, as the huge room had no doors or holes, save the one I had made in the ceiling. I shuddered with a sudden chill. Again my superstitions exposed themselves, and I risked a glance over my shoulder, half expecting the husk of a corpse to be rising from the very grave, stretching out long, bony fingers to take me by the throat.

It was gone! My heart leaped in my chest, and I spun in circles, shining the lantern this way and that. This was not possible! Stony hands caught me by the shirt, and I was instantly raised from the ground and spun roughly around to face my attacker. Dark hollows glared at me from where the eyes should have been, and dried sinews stretched to allow its gaping jaws to open and stretch wider than what should have been possible, revealing long rows of jagged, yellowed teeth.

In my inexpressible horror, some part of my brain was still working while the rest was paralyzed with utter terror. I noticed a shape in the darkness, a gold accented arquebus, the precursor to the muskets of almost a century before, lying abandoned a mere few feet away. The ramrod was sticking from the barrel, there was the slightest chance it had been thrown or torn away just as its former owner had just finished loading it. If I could free myself, it was the one weapon I saw that offered the slightest chance. But what could mortal weapons do to one already muerto?

The corpse pulled me in closer, dried tissues cracked and crumbled in its arms. It bellowed, impossibly loud, sending forth a cloud of grave rot and dust from its cavernous maw. My eyes locked on the teeth I was sure would close around my head in mere moments, I seemed unable to move, paralyzed, then all broke loose in a lightning bolt's time and I kicked out with every last bit of my strength, knocking its rotting jaw sideways and tearing myself free from its bony grasp.

I hit the floor hard, but didn't feel it, and scrambled away from the terror beyond my wildest nightmares. The corpse crackled and crunched as the bones seemed to right themselves, then it lurched towards me. Some instinct took me, and I froze again, my fingers inches from the ancient rifle. The unholy relic froze too, as if it could not see me, and I remembered its eyes were mere caves into its skull, perhaps it could not see me.

The creature waved its head from side to side, sniffing the air audibly. It was trying to find me by scent. I stretched, my bones straining out of their sockets to try and lay a finger on the rifle. There. The rifle scraped against the stone floor, and the corpse roared and sprang forward with long, crooked strides, straight for me. Abandoning all hopes of evasion, I gathered the long firearm in my arms and strove to pull back the hammer. There was no flint, just a tiny piece of dried out cord with a blackened end. Fire!

The creature was almost upon me. It was too late, but I snatched at my shirt pocket for the matches I carried. Bony hands reached out for me. I struck a match against the floor. It burst into flame, then promptly fizzled out. The creature seemed to sense the flame, and flinched back. I struck another, throwing it at the monster, and it snatched its hand back as if burned. It roared at me.

"Miguel! Step away!"

Father Cortez appeared in the opening in the ceiling. He was flanked by two men of the village, wearing black cloaks. Father Cortez carried a gigantic sword on his back, even though it now gleamed like the sun I instantly recognized it as the one I had found rusted and abandoned in the caves and brought to him a year before. He leapt from the opening all the way to the floor in one graceful move, and drew the sword. The hilt and handguard glittered brightly in the lantern light, and the priest seemed transformed. He moved with a grace and athleticism as I had never seen before, he circled the creature with the movements of a skilled swordsman.

"Miguel, foolish boy! Get out of here!"

The other two men dropped a rope to the ground, and slid down it. They carried torches and heavy skins across their backs, filled with sloshing liquid.

The creature lumbered towards father, who spun gracefully out of the way slicing deep with the sword as he moved. The monster howled in rage and pain.

"Up the rope, my son, and quickly!"

One of the men lifted me onto the rope, and I climbed swiftly, looking back all the while over my shoulder. Father Cortez advanced, keeping the point of his sword between him and the creature. The other two men sprung forward, swinging their torches. Father shouted "No!" but it was too late, the creature seemed to snatch one of them out of the very air, carrying him off into the shadows. The other man froze, quivering. The creature had moved almost too fast to be seen. I kept climbing.

Father Cortez snatched the torch out of the terrified man's hand, and advanced warily into the darkness just outside the circle of my lantern. His torch cast a flickering light which revealed the limp form of a man being held by the creature, whose jagged teeth were sunk deep into his throat, nearly severing the head. The monster sucked greedily, and while he drank deep of his victim's lifeblood, the creature's own mouldering flesh seemed to take on life of its own, growing more supple, filling in, one eye swelling and then filling with a bright, gleaming blue iris. It shot up at me. Una vampiro! I had heard the tales, meant to frighten young children and the simple, but never did I believe! And here it was, an unholy creature, cursed by God, banished from heaven, and it was staring straight at me!

Even Father Cortez seemed shaken by the sight, but he lunged at the creature with his sword. The vampiro dropped his victim like an empty wineskin, and grabbed the point of Father's elegant sword. The Priest and the fiend locked in battle. Father Cortez leaned all his strength into his sword, sliding the point through the creature's grasp. The vampiro locked down on the blade with both hands, but still the blade slid through, black blood oozing down the edge as it got closer and closer to his heart. The flesh was still closing and swelling to life in the dead man's face, wisps of whitened hair becoming a long, full, golden beard.

The priest grimaced, sweat pouring from his face as he put all of his strength into driving the sword home. The fiend roared, and ripped the blade sideways out of father's hands, where it clattered across the floor. The priest barely dodged a swipe from the sharp claws, and snatched a crucifix from his robe. He held it up and the creature shrunk back, lifting his arm as if to block the very sight of it.

The priest bravely strode forward, muttering a fervent prayer under his breath. The vampiro retreated, grudgingly, bellowing out his rage so loud I wanted to let go of the rope and cover my ears. Father advanced in spite of it all, only pausing in his prayer long enough to call back to me over his shoulder.

"Get out of here my son! Vaya con Dios!"

I was frozen, watching the spectacle. The vampiro slammed his fists against the stone wall in frustration and rage, sending splinters of rock flying across the room. Some of the shrapnel hit Father Cortez in the eyes, causing him to falter and drop the crucifix. Time slowed to a crawl. The fiend charged. I let go of the rope. Father Cortez threw himself to the ground, groping blindly for the only weapon left to him, the fallen crucifix. In doing so, he saved his life, if only for a few moments.

The creature's fist whistled through the air above father's head as he leaped past with blinding speed. I hit the ground. Rolling up, I snatched up the ancient rifle and then the lantern with my other hand. Father had gotten hold of the cross and was bringing it up when the vampiro materialized back out of the shadows and knocked it away. The crucifix spun out into the darkness. I brought the lantern around in a wide arc, smashing glass and burning oil onto the breech of the old rifle.

It exploded. In my haste, I had forgotten the loading rod was still in the barrel, and as burning powder forever marked my face, the loading rod pierced the creature through, pinning it to the wall. I fell, and the world spun in circles as I hit the ground. Sounds seemed to come through water and from far away. Rough hands grabbed me up, in between beats of my heart I heard Father Cortez's voice urging the terrified man, now unfrozen, to get me to safety.

I drooped and sagged, strapped to the mans back, and watched the priest below with a skin in each hand splashing liquid around the cavern as we climbed the rope. The hellish fiend struggled to free itself from the rod piercing its ribcage, reaching out as if it could somehow stretch its hand up and snatch me back. Its teeth gleamed white now, and they gnashed together as the vampiro screamed out its rage to the very heavens. Father splashed the last of the skins on the unholy demon itself, then turned to look up at me as he picked up the torch.

"I love you, my son. My own son," were the last words I heard my earthly father speak to me.

He was smiling, as the man carrying me reached the top and pulled us out of the hole.

Father dropped the torch, and the cavern erupted in flame."

CHAPTER 7

"So, with tears still in my eyes, I was sent off to Rome. It was only there, and years later, that I would enter a most secret and ancient order, and be educated in the many ways the forces of darkness assail the world of mortals. We are the first and last line of defense against the unholy plague that now threatens this land, and indeed, the whole world."

"Sounds like pretty on'ry stuff you're messing with here padre." I said, rolling a smoke. If'n I hadn't seen it with my own two eyes, I'd be guessing the priest had been drinking the local tequila for too long, but as it was, how could I but believe him?

"I thought the danger was over, and so did the church, that my father's sacrifice had extinguished it once and for all. But when I heard of several disturbing events from a...friend of the order here in Rio de Sangre, I knew it was not over. The evil had returned. So I was sent here to investigate, and see if it was true.

Our resources are scarce, and the church has only so many warriors to send into battle. You see, when the church first arrived on these shores, the Aztecs worshipped just such monsters as you have encountered today. They kept them pacified with human sacrifices on an unimaginable scale. They thought their masters were gods, in reality, they were being farmed like cattle.

When Cortez landed in what was then known as Espania Nuevo, New Spain, many centuries ago, my ancestors on both sides warred in these territories, losing countless lives in the battle for men's souls. History no longer knows the truth of what happened, indeed at the time the Spanish authorities sent over 1,400 soldiers to arrest Cortez for going beyond his orders. They thought it was a mad search for gold, but he had learned of what plagues this land, and as any good man would, he defied the powers of both earth and hell to see it extinguished. He failed.

One of his own betrayed him, and drove him from the land. He returned to Spain to be greeted like a hero, for discovering and conquering new lands in the name of the crown, but they refused to heed his warnings. His pleadings fell on deaf ears, and the princes of the earth hastened to send more flesh as fodder for these old "gods". He was later accused of great cruelty to the people of New Spain, no one would believe those he slaughtered were the very minions of El Diablo.

But the church knew, and we have been fighting a secret battle in these lands ever since. A battle we thought we had won. The situation here though, is worse than even we anticipated. No one that comes here leaves. I have been unable to send word. The vampiros have coerced the local populace into serving them, and what else can they do? They could take shelter in the sanctuary, but we would all quickly starve. So the villagers offer the lives of the desperados and bandits who are cursed enough to take shelter in this town. In this way they save their lives and the lives of their children, at least for a time. I have tried to dissuade them, but they are too terrified to heed my words. They will not fight."

Billy Joe started cursing the villagers at that, for a low-down pack of scoundrels, and that was sayin' it the polite way. The words he used were the kind a body shouldn't ever use in a church, and even if I hadn't darkened the door of one in a coon's age, I rapped him one across the beater to shut him up. I might be a lowdown outlaw, but every fella' knows there's some lines that ought not to be crossed.

"You must understand." the Padre pleaded, "The people here do not wish to do these things, but they have no choice.

Their families, their children, will be slaughtered in turn if they do not offer the blood of those who, if you will forgive me for saying so, have done much more to deserve their fate than these simple people. Maria came to me in tears, and told me what she had done. Leaving you down there, in the darkness with those things, I can understand, you must be... angry with her, but please, you must not hold it against her!"

I stuttered, at a loss for words. Since nothing that was likely to come out of my mouth was fit for church and all, I just stamped my foot against the marble floor and bit my tongue 'til it bled. Just the same, even with all that was done, I couldn't help but be just a bit affected that Maria had at least shed a tear for me.

A lot of men died without having a woman to cry over them, even if it wasn't sayin' much. Darn it all, the Maker must've thought makin' men a bunch of durn fools over any gal with a pretty smile was a real hoot; 'cause despite my better judgment and all sense, I just couldn't hold it against her. I needed to get out of this church, 'cause stronger language was needed given my feelings on the matter, and I needed a good cuss. Durn it.

"You in the Church!" A familiar voice rang out. A voice I had come to despise.

The windows on either side of the door to the church were unstained, letting in bright clean light. I stood up on my toes to see out. Major Wilhelm sat his horse in the middle of the street, surrounded by his men. It was my first good look at the man.

"You bandits come on out of there, and face the justice you deserve, by order of the U.S. Army!" he bellowed in rich, mellifluent tones, stroking his blonde chin beard.

"Nobody in here Major, just a few pious churchgoing folk, prayin' the rosary and such! Them bandits done got away, you might be able to ketch'um if you leave right quick, hear they took off going northaway's to the fort to turn themselves in!" was my less than convincing reply. He

53

must have known we were in here anyhow, and if a body doesn't have some fun once in a while, not much sense in livin', or so I see it.

The major smiled with bright, perfect white teeth. "I'm giving you men the chance to come out and face your judgement honorably! Throw down your guns, and surrender. You're outnumbered, and out of options. You know it, and I know it. Now, I'd surely be dismayed if I had to burn down that holy building, just to cleanse it from the presence of rapscallions such as you! I declare, if you try my patience, you will find I shall be much less lenient than I am currently being. Come out with your hands up, and tell us where the gold is, and perhaps we shall spare your lives."

"Clay, what's a rapscallion?" Billy asked, and I near burst out laughing, in spite of the situation. Tense times like these tend to make me feel 'specially like laughing for some reason, perhaps I'm touched in the head.

"Tell you what Major, since you're a military man, I'll lend you the courtesy of a counter-offer. You all throw down your guns and leave town right now, and I won't track you to the ends of the earth, and gun down each and every one of you on behalf of my friends you done killed! I'm Clay Wilder, and I'm hell on wheels for those of you that don't know me, and I see some of you do."

When I said my name, I saw a few of the men glance around some at their fellows, it was a name they knew and did not like the thought of stacking up against. A newspaper out east had taken to calling me the wild and wilder western prince of thieves, and publishing ridiculously embellished tales of my exploits and adventures, and perhaps made me out to be just a bit of a gunslick. That sort of reputation had caused me some trouble in the past with greenhorns trying to make a name for themselves, it was time I used it to my benefit.

"As an added bonus Major, if y'all clear on out of here on the double-quick, I won't have to open up with this here

Gatling gun, and spill a bunch of brass all over the inside of this here church.

Now that gave them pause. A naked bluff to be sure, but I didn't have a lot of ideas, and I needed time to give a few thoughts and plans a chance to smolder and burst into flame.

The Major set his teeth for a moment, then spat and motioned to someone off to the side. My toes were starting to ache from standing on them so long.

They brought out someone in a familiar looking dress. Her hands were tied in front of her with rope, a black hood covering her face.

The Major leaned over in the saddle to rip the hood off with a flourish. The buzzards!

Maria stood tall and erect in the bright sun, her hair spilling over her face. Her chin was high, a defiant set to her pouty lips. Her eyes were fierce and hard, edged by long dark lashes. She was beautiful.

"Fine and dandy then, if you refuse to come out and surrender your persons, we'll be forced to start administering justice to those who've sheltered and housed you. Of course, you may end this all right now, and leave these people in peace, but if not..."

I knew what I would do the minute my feet started for the door. No use thinking about it, somethin' (and I hoped to flesh that plan out a mite), somethin' just had to be done. I couldn't let someone else pay the price for the trouble I'd brought to this town, even with the history me and that gal had between us, and I only hoped she'd been chosen at random, because she was a pretty young thing, and not because the major somehow sensed that this was the one gal in the world that had some kind of magical power sent by the devil himself to twist my guts all up in knots.

"What are you doing Clay?" Billy Joe gasped as I pushed open the wide church doors. Dust swirled lazily around my boots as I threw the doors open and stood there for a moment. It all must have looked rather dramatic, but the odds were they wouldn't gun me down right there and then, not just yet, and after the darkness of the church, my eyes needed to adjust to the light thrown by the setting sun. I suppose it was a good thing that churches are built facing east, since that put the sun directly behind me, a small enough advantage when facing a whole company of soldiers, but I'd take anything I could get at this moment.

A broad smile spread across the dainty officer's face, his men fanned out to either side. I walked easily down the steps, trying not to let the utter certainty I was a dead man show on my features. Slowly, easily, I took the makings of a smoke out of my shirt pocket, and rolled myself one as I walked down the street to meet my doom. I was hell on wheels with my pair of six guns, but I desperately wished for a rifle, even if that would only allow me to take a few more to the grave with me.

The soldiers glanced nervously about as I approached. They weren't stupid, clearly they had me dead to rights. Many of them must have been hardened veterans of countless border skirmishes, Indian wars, and hunts for desperados such as I. But none of them were counting on a lightly armed man to just come strolling out to meet them, with a smile on his face, appearing not to have a care in the world. Clearly, something else was going on, and that's just what I wanted them to think. Their uncertainty would buy me time, instead of moving to seize me, they eyed the rooftops and surrounding windows warily, expecting some kind of trick. A brilliant plan would hit me like a flash of lightning, any moment now.

"Pleased to make yer acquaintance, Major," I mouthed around the cigarette, striking a match on my belt and taking a few puffs.

"Your men seem a might skittish, if you don't mind my sayin' so. They worried about somethin'?"

The major didn't seem to know what to make of my easy manner, clearly, he had the upper hand here, but he'd doubtless studied tactics and strategy in some fancy college out east, and everything I was doing were classic signs of a ruse. Meanwhile, I was still waitin' on that plan.

It was an awkward moment, me standing there a'grinnin' in the street, the major sitting tall and utterly nonplussed in the saddle. Now he had me, he seemed at a loss as to just what to do with me. He recovered after a moment, said, "I accept your surrender, drop your guns man, and tell us where you've hidden the gold."

Taking a drag of the smoke, I took my time about answering.

"Well, Major, I can't help but ask, just what are you planning on doin' with it anyway? I mean, hey, you've won and all, might as well tell a feller just what's going to become of the treasure he worked so hard to steal."

The Major laughed. "I've decided I like you, Wilder. Its a shame I'll have to execute you and your men, of course. Oh, very well. You see, that shipment of gold was never a payroll at all. The army has been receiving reports from my command for quite some time, as to a buildup of Mexican forces at the border, repeated Indian raids, and of course, assaults from gangs of unsavory bandits on nearby towns. A part of that is certainly true, but then, I was faced with the problem of having plenty of resources at my disposal to crush any threats to the area, but a great dearth of funds for my retirement. You see, as glamorous as military life may seem, I am simply not paid what I am worth. I come from a large and wealthy family, though lately my father's fortunes have...waned somewhat, and he needs quite a bit of money to secure the cooperation of the political class in Washington, and secure the contract for a railroad which is to be built along the border. Now, that railroad cannot be built without enough security in the area to vouchsafe the people's investment, and furthermore, my family needs the money to buy the cooperation of those funding the project. Now, what better than to secure such resources from those who require them? All in all, the politicians get their own money back, and they always make sure to get a large cut of the government's largess for themselves, so is anyone really harmed? Well, other than you, no one. You certainly built a fire under my plans, but its all turned out for the better, I must say. You and your "gang" take the credit, or rather the blame, for the loss of the shipment, which, sad to say, shall have been unrecoverable, no doubt hidden somewhere before your demise at the hands of my brave soldiers. This will save me months of falsifying expenditures to build a fort which will be a mere shell of what shall exist on paper, and likely a medal for bringing to justice such a disreputable band of desperados such as yourselves. And who knows? The Army may yet find it even more necessary to send additional funds for this fort, since what further proof could be required for its necessity than recent events? At the end of it, Wilder, I owe you my thanks, you've helped make my lies a reality. Don't look so perturbed man, I do plan to put in my reports how you and your men resisted to the last, which will make it unnecessary to come up with a transcript of interrogation, and you'll be remembered with more inflated stories in the newspapers all across the country. We all win, more or less. Well, some more than less." The major twirled the end of his mustache, clearly quite pleased with himself. All I felt was a deep and burning anger inside me. I could only hope Maria hadn't let on she knew English, or she'd be as dead as I would be in a moment. No flash of lightning came from the heavens, outlining a devious plan that would allow me to both escape and get Maria to safety. But the major in his hubris had overlooked one thing, desperate men do desperate things. I would gun him down right there, and make my stand against the rest, and hope they cut me down quick.

The major must have seen the change in my eyes, because his smile disappeared and his face went white. He froze, realizing there was no way his men could gun me down in time, I was right next to him, and in firing at me he could easily be killed as well.

It was a long moment, The Major frozen still with fear, my fingers itching for the feel of wood on steel, and the smell of gunsmoke would soon fill the air. I imagined an eternity of kicking the major's prim and proper backside all over the depths of hell from one side to the other, and it didn't seem so bad after all.

Somehow, I was aware of a drop of sweat falling from the brow of the soldier closest to me, and it seemed like it took forever to hit the dust. Now.

My gun cleared leather as if of its own volition; in a fraction of a second I had a clear picture of the bead resting between the major's wide eyes. And in that moment the thought hit me which should've been obvious all along. I slashed with the barrel of the Colt, hitting the officer right across the temple. He went limp as he tumbled from the saddle, straight into my waiting arms. I heaved him up so he was a shield between me and most of his men, but I was still surrounded.

"Nobody move or this sorry vulture gets his ears cleaned!" I shouted, and stuffed the muzzle of the Colt in the appropriate place so they'd get the sense of my threat. The soldiers backed off a pace, but the large bores of their .45-70s followed me as steadily as did their eyes.

I shuffled back, struggling with the dead weight of the unconscious Major, but it would only be a matter of time before someone tried to take a shot, and all hell would break loose.

"Take him men, just don't hit the Commander!" One of the sergeants shouted, taking charge. I was still surrounded on all sides, my goose was cooked. With any luck, I'd be able to take Willhelm with me, a play-mate for an eternity of fire. The very thought meant I'd go out with a smile.

"Stop!"

Maria stepped in front of me, spreading her hands wide.

"What the hell you doin' gal? Get the hell outta the way, you'll be cut down too!" I spat, but she just glared at me. The men behind me moved in, but she stepped around so she was between me and them.

"I owe you a debt Clay. I don't know how you survived, but you don't know the anguish I felt at what I did to you. Please forgive me. This is the only way I know how to atone for what I did. Go, escape while you can!"

"I ain't got time to argue right now gal, just step aside, these men and I have business to attend to. 'Sides, this town's gonna have enough trouble as it is, without their womenfolk getting killed and some villagers shootin' back, and then they'll just suffer all the worse."

"So you will take them all on single-handed si? The rough, tough, gringo vaquero, come to save me with his big guns and bigger mouth. And then what senor big-shot? I have looked out for this village my whole life, since I was a girl. What do you know of what we need? You brought these men here."

"Like I said-"

"Quiet, you silly man. You have no idea the trouble I have gone to so that we could keep some measure of peace and safety in this village, our prison. You have ruined every-thing. At least have the decency to stand quiet when some-one tries to save your miserable life."

The sun was melting away over the horizon and the soldiers crept in along with the lengthening shadows of the coming night. Even if Maria was determined to use herself as a human shield, I wasn't going anywhere. We all pointed our guns at each other, me and the soldiers, and now Billy Joe, who burst out the door of the church with a six gun in each hand.

"Anyone moves I'll fill him so full of lead he'll...he'll... die deadern' a skunk!" was Billy Joe's addition to the con-versation. He never was much good at desperado talk. Or much else.

Somewhere, an eagle screamed in the sky. At any moment, the world could erupt in smoke and flame. I'd been in tense standoffs before, but none that matched the one I was stuck in now, right here in Mexico. We were all gonna' die.

CHAPTER 8

The sun was going down, burning bright red, casting the clouds purple as they lined the distant hills. Giant pillars of rock stretched to the sky like jagged teeth, the adobe buildings gave back the heat of the day as the cool breeze of evening began its sweep through the town, rustling brush and clothing. Maria's skirts fluttered in the wind, and in spite of myself I couldn't help but risk a glance at the well turned out ankle, briefly revealed.

It was four guns against ten times that number, and one of mine was still pressed against the unconscious Major's head. I was a hopeful man, by nature, but there was no way out of this one, the odds were just too great. May as well open the ball.

"Y'all weren't gonna throw this here party without me, were ya?"

Like the angel of death himself, ashen and drawn, Whiskey Jack Watson appeared on the veranda of the hotel, two bandoliers of shells over his shoulders and a double barrel shotgun in each hand. He was pale as death, but he stood straight and tall, and his voice boomed over the crowd of assembled soldiers.

"Looks like yer' in a bit of a pickle down there Clay."

"I could use some company, that's for sure." I drawled back, trying to keep my eyes on all the soldiers at once.

"Well, we rode the hoot owl trail together some years now, ain't we Clay? My death's comin' for me, I can feel it. Might as well make it count for somethin'."

With no further comment Whiskey Jack opened up on the soldiers, and them at him. Billy Joe walked forward off the church steps, snapping shots, and I caught Maria by the arm and flung her down.

One soldier swung on me, and I cut loose with the Colts, he dropped like a stone. A second blazed a shot past my ear, somewhere behind me, but Jack's shotgun roared above my head, and he fell with a thud. Jack twisted as the slugs tore into him, but caught himself on the railing and took up the other shotgun and returned fire. Two more soldiers bounced and rolled in the dust, jagged wounds across their chests.

My guns barked hellfire and brimstone for a few short seconds, then ran dry and I fetched up the major's ivory handled Schofield. I shot it dry, and two more men wouldn't see the coming night. Billy Joe took a volley of bullets all at once, and went down twitching and firing off his final round into his own boot.

Jack was soaking up lead like he did liquor, as if he'd made up his mind he was already dead and so the bullets couldn't do any more damage. The soldiers took cover as Jack fetched up a levergun out of nowhere and set to, dropping man after man in his tracks. I made the last two shots with my derringer count, turning a younger man's face into a messy hole as he charged me with an empty rifle, swinging it like a club.

I grabbed Maria by a foot and tugged her back with me and my hostage into an empty store. Dumping them both through the door, I dove clear of the street and gathered up my weapons. Major Wilhelm shook his head and sat up, with a confused look on his face. I didn't want him awake and movin' around just yet, so I balled up a fist and let him have it, and he went back to sleep right quick. He was a lot more manageable that way. Refilling my guns, I kept an eye on the scene outside.

Whiskey Jack leapt from the railing and hit the ground like he was feeling no pain. He was striding forward calm and easy as if he'd been on his way to the saloon, 'cept he was leveling his six guns and burning down man after man as they scrambled to take cover behind barrels and buildings. Jack took two more rounds from a sergeant with an old horse pistol, then raised his Colt and shot the man dead through his left eye. Ol' Whiskey just stood there in the middle of the street, riddled with bullets, looking for targets. Lord help me, I couldn't just leave him there to die alone.

My guns reloaded, I ducked down as a bullet cracked against the window, showering me with chunks of plaster. I came out of the store guns blazing, hollering who-knows-what, straight into a volley of gunfire. The first round hit me in the calf, and all I felt was a strong tug on my leg, but I lost my balance and tumbled forward, rounds whistling through the air above me like shrieking harpies.

Jack took another slug through the chest, and staggered a mite, then coughed up a torrent of blood into the street. He paused a moment, as if transfixed by the sight of all his own lifeblood just settin' there, mingling with the dust. Another round caught him and he fell like a stone to his knees, and keeled over, dead.

Little puffs of smoke and dirt kicked up all around me as I became the last and only target left, and I backpedaled, snapping off a wild shot here and there as I went. There must be an angel what looks after poor dumb fools such as me, 'cause I made it back into the shop without another scratch. Another volley of slugs came pouring through the window, but I kept low and covered Maria's body with my own. I reloaded my Colts and the Schofield, my derringer, and then dragged Maria and then the hostage back behind the thick wood counter of the shop. The incoming fire died down some, but bullets were still coming through pretty regular, and I stayed down.

As long as they kept firing at the building the others weren't charging through the door, a situation I was happy with, for now. Just as I finished tying my kerchief above my boot, which at least slowed the bleeding, a box behind the counter caught my eye. Two double barreled shotguns had been cut down to near nothing, but refinished and refined by an expert craftsman. The pistols had short handles with no stock left, and the barrels weren't longer than eight inches. Probably the solution found by some desperado who either couldn't see worth a darn or couldn't shoot straight, and who met the same fate I almost did in the caverns beneath the town.

A few boxes of shotgun shells rested beside the box, and they were just the thing I needed now. I had desperately wished for a rifle, but the extremely abbreviated barrels would allow me to darn near fill the doorway with buckshot each trigger pull, and perhaps that would be enough to take the starch out of any attempt they might make to storm the store in force.

Loading the double barrels quickly, I set my own Colts in my lap and scooted around to face the door with one in each hand.

It would be dark soon, and I was already starting to feel the wound in my leg, all my limbs felt kind of weak and shaky.

Maria came to. She spat a rapid discourse in Spanish at yours truly, none of which sounded complimentary in the least. What a lady.

When she was finished, she crawled over to me and began poking and prodding, finally discovering the wound in my leg, which began another round of rapid fire Spanish. I began to protest when she ripped off my kerchief, but to my surprise she smacked me across the face and put a finger to her lips. Like I said, feisty.

Maria kept low but searched the store until she found a bottle of that God-awful tequila and splashed it liberally over my wound. It hurt so bad it would have been a fair trade if I shot her in return. I gasped back the pain and gritted my teeth, managing to keep silent.

"We've got to get out of here before dark!" She hissed at me in English, and I didn't need to ask why.

"You killed some of the monsters. How Stupid! Now they will want revenge. As soon as it gets dark, they will come out, and kill us all! Estupido! What were you thinking?!"

"Well, little lady, if a certain someone hadn't thrown me right into that nest of vipers, I might have been able to live and let live, and right now I'd be well on my way somewheres, anywheres else!"

Maria sighed, blew a strand of hair out of her face as she rebandaged my wound, proper-like.

"You are right of course. I should not have done it. But if I did not, my family would be killed. The entire village would be killed! We are...hostages in our own homes. We cannot leave, we cannot escape. We have no hope. And now we will all die. Better, I think, not to have taken others with us."

She punctuated each sentence with sharp, hard movements, and that meant she was playing holy havoc with the gaping wound on my leg. It hurt something fierce.

"There, it is not so bad. You will live, at least until they come. I cannot think we have much time left. I can only think now of how much I have left undone, now that it is too late to do it. I have lived my whole life under the shadow of these demons, content merely to keep my people safe, the demons placated, all with the blood of evil men. I do not know how people live elsewhere, but I hear the talk. Elegant dances and great balls. Traveling to different places. Beautiful green fields, full of life. Far away mountains, crystal clear rivers. So many places that people see and travel, but my place is here. My place always will be here, so long as the demons have a hold on us. If only the people would fight...but no. They will never fight. They are content to live in the shadow of darkness, so long as they remain unharmed. And so I do what I must to give them that chance.

When I was just a girl, my brother would come home from his work, late at night, and tell me stories he had heard. He said they came from books in town. I seldom went into this village. My brother worked to support us. Our mother was a woman shamed and alone, my brother the child of some wandering vaquero. At least, that is what people said. My mother did what was...necesidad to support him when he was very little, which is how I am told I came into being. A child of shame. These people I now protect looked at me with disgust, if they saw me at all. But my brother grew, and made my mother stay home, working like una perro to support us, with whatever work he could find to put his hand to.

But no matter how hard he had worked or how hungry we were, he would tuck me into my blankets and tell me the stories. A knight saving a princess from a terrible dragon. A house in the woods, make of sugar and candy. Fearsome monsters and evil witches, but all defeated by a hero, with shining armor and a white horse. Always the stories ended with felices para siempre, a happily ever after.

I used to dream of a knight, a tall, handsome knight in armor, riding a great horse, and wielding a shining sword. He would defeat the monsters that live in the caverns below, and sweep me off my feet.

But I am a woman grown now, and I know there are no heroes, and no one is coming to save me. I will never know another life beyond this place. I will never wear a beautiful dress, never dance at a ball, never know true love. There will be no happily ever after, not for me."

Maria wrapped up the remaining bandages, her dark eyes moist and sad.

Sometimes, in the worst of times, the heavens conspire to speed up the natural course of things between a man and a woman. She needed comfort, she was afraid, she was fierce. There was only one thing I could think of to do.

I grabbed her face and kissed her for all I was worth.

We just stood there for a moment after, staring into each others eyes, breathless. She slapped me. Then she kissed me back.

Fiesty.

CHAPTER 9

Darkness settled on the streets of Rio de Sangre like a predatory bird, unfurling dark wings to blot out the last of the remaining sun.

I kept watch on the window, and Maria sulked in the corner, occasionally muttering under her breath bits and pieces of a running commentary in Spanish, but I gathered it was something along the lines of how stupid it was to be trapped in a general store, surrounded by soldiers, with a pack o' angry hellspawn prowling somewheres underneath the town. I cupped my smoke, drawing on it gently and keeping it well away from the window. The soldiers seemed to be waiting, all was still and quiet in the gathering dark. I'd half expected them to charge by now, but the bloodshed earlier in the day must've taken some starch out of their trousers, and perhaps, they didn't care much more for their commander than I did. Major Jonas Willhelm of the United States Army, murderer, defrauder, and betrayer of his country's trust, sat bound and gagged in the corner, looking alternately sullen and enraged. He was my bargaining chip to get Maria and I the heck out of Dodge. Make that Rio de Sangre, Dodge City would be a welcome sight about now.

There were two things that could happen here. Either the soldiers would wait until the darkness finished settling to make a surprise attack, or they would wait me out, counting on time and the long night to wear me down and frazzle my nerves, so's they could take me unawares. Either course of action would be deadly for Maria and I. In truth, the soldiers were the lesser part of my worries. I wouldn't show it in front of Maria, but the thought of being in this town overnight with those creatures made a feller plumb nervous.

There was a rustling noise and whispered voices from the darkness in the buildings across the street.

"Halt! Who goes ther-AAACK!"

"What's that? Bill! Where's yer haid?! Oh by the stars! NOOOOOoooo!"

A sudden rush of gunfire and short screams, intermingled with the sound of something whipping through the buildings like the wind screamed through the arroyos, and then all fell silent except for a faint gurgling. They were here. My blood ran cold. My fingers tightened on the double barrels.

"Clay!" Maria shouted, then Willhelm's fist cracked against her skull, and she tumbled to the floor. The Major had gotten free of his bonds while I was distracted, perhaps he'd been working on them the whole time while I was watching the window and Maria was sulking about our doom instead of keeping an eye on the prisoner.

Willhelm came at me swinging a piece of wood from the floor, his eyes desperate, but I ducked aside and swung like I meant it. My fist caught him in the forehead, sending bolts of pain shooting up my arm, and then Willhelm crashed to the floor, down, but not out. He struck out with the make-shift club, catching me across the shins, and in spite of my-self I rolled forward, crashing to the floor. Willhelm saw his opportunity, and ran for it. I raised my gun, but he was out the door and it would have been a wasted shot.

Hauling my carcass up, I leapt out after him, then drew up short. A creature from the nightmares of damned souls stood in the street, holding Willhelm's twitching body in the air, impaled on a twisted, pale arm. The creature lurched forward with impossibly wide jaws, burying them in the major's neck. As the thing sucked greedily at the wound, it turned a bright red eye to glare at me.

Sometimes, discretion is the better part of valor, and I suddenly remembered I had other fish to fry. Backpedaling through the door, I gathered Maria up and tossed her over my shoulder. There was no other exit to the store. I stepped back out into the street, keeping my back to the wall and every inch of distance I could muster between the feeding monster and me.

The creature tossed Willhelm's limp and drained body aside like he was a rag doll and shot forward in front of me, pausing to crouch and roar like a lion. Those jagged teeth, stained red with blood, framed a black hole that seemed a thousand miles deep. It looked like the door to hell.

There would be no running, not with how fast these things moved. I didn't figurr much on my chances of nego-tiatin' a truce, neither.

Fortunately, I had two double barrel shotgun-pistols to roar back with. I lifted one and pulled both triggers, aimed straight at the creature's maw, and watched the upper half of his jaw and head disappear. The body reeled in the street, slashing out this way and that for a short moment before col-lapsing in a pile of smoldering embers. The wind seemed to come out of nowhere to blow it away. Ashes to ashes.

I didn't need any prodding, and grabbing Maria by the hand, we took off running down the street. Perhaps luck would be a lady tonight, and I could make the stables. Them things was fast, but my steeldust could give the wind what for when it came to runnin', and we'd just see who was the faster. Then I remembered the last time I'd reached the stables, dreaming of escape, just to find my horse was gone. Blazes!

Thumbing fresh shells into the pistol as I went, my mind raced in hopes of chancing upon another one o' them bril-liant plans. A dark shadow whipped into view at the end of the street, and I turned and sprinted down an alley to the right. Another shadow blocked my path. I turned to flee again, but now that entrance was blocked as well with a dark silhouette, only the moonlight served to show the source of my impending doom. I was trapped by the things at either end of the alley, bloodthirsty hellbeasts bent on revenge and the taste of Maria's and my own blood. Bring back the soldiers already.

I turned sideways, raising the double barrels to cover each direction. Keeping an eye on each was another story altogether. I could only make quick, furtive glances left and right, and as fast as these things were they'd be able to move on me while I was eyeballing the wrong way. But the shadows didn't move, just stood there, hemming me in.

"Disappointing..." came an impossibly smooth voice, seemingly out of nowhere. My head snapped about in every direction.

An exasperated sigh. "Up here, outlaw."

My eyes shot up. Atop the building in front of me stood a figure out of the 16th century. Dressed like a Spanish conquistador, complete with rapier, neat blonde beard and mustache, and frilly, colorful doublet.

"I must say I had expected more. My...children told me how they suffered at the hands of a mere mortal, I thought, surely, this man must be something special. Indeed, you have even slain another of my brood tonight. Perhaps your appearance is deceiving, and you are more than you seem. But just looking at you, I very much doubt it. I am Juan Antonio de la Vega, second in command of all Spanish forces in the Vice Royalty of the New Spain. I would say I am pleased to make your acquaintance but...tell me, what is your name?"

Now, the reddish glow behind his eyes was surely terrifying, but after all, whoever this guy was; and I had a notion he was the same feller from the sad story Father Cortez had spun for me, he was dressed like a dandy and sayin' some mighty uncomplimentary things toward yours truly, and that got my dander up a bit.

"I'm Clay Wilder, and I'll send you back from whence you came, hellspawn!" I added the "whence" bit from some play I'd seen when a traveling theater troupe made the rounds through a cow town I'd been hidin' out in some years back. Thought it sounded right dramatic, at that.

The man atop the building just laughed, a cultured, rich mocking sound seemed to echo all around me. Well, we'd see how well he'd chortle with a mouth full of buckshot. That sort of thing tends to gum up the works some.

I lifted one of the pistols and fired, straight at the man's face. In the flash of powder I saw clearly he was already gone. I looked around wildly, searching for my target.

"Right here, Mr. Wilder."

Behind me! I started to spin, lashing out with the barrel, but there was nothing. Another long, throaty laugh echoed off the walls, seeming to come from everywhere and no-where. Downright creepy, the way he done that.

The two vampires on each end of the alley charged. I dropped the empty double barrel and snatched out my Colt, snapping shots down one end of the alley while giving the other both barrels. The vampires staggered, and I dropped the other empty double and commenced to raisin' hell. In less than a second or two, thick gunsmoke obscured my view of either, and I slammed my Colts into their holsters and drew out the Schofield, running back the way I come, Maria still limp over my shoulder. Better stay asleep, gal. It'll be easier than way. No pain.

I come a'runnin' out of the smoke smack dab into the still reeling vampire. They didn't look nothin' like their boss, more like some kind of twisted thing out of the brimstone below, all pale and gnarled, with those large, jagged teeth. The creature roared and stepped forward, the holes in its chest closing themselves up and spitting out the soft lead pellets as he came. Downright discouraging, that. I replaced the buckshot he was shedding with a slug through his throat, and grinned with satisfaction as he collapsed back against the wall, coughing and snarling. Looked downright uncom-fortable for him, so to help matters along I put two more into his skull, and he dropped like a stone. I hoped he stayed there.

Running on with Maria, she came to suddenly, startled, and for a moment I thought the vampire behind us had caught up and leapt on my back. The little gal put up quite a fuss, pounding her small hard fists on my back, and somehow catching me one in the kisser with one of her boots, though I couldn't figure how she managed that trick.

"Sueltame demonio!" she shrieked.

"Maria! It's me! I've got you!"

I set her petite form down and lifted the Schofield in a hurry, as the monster behind us appeared out of the smoke, stumbling all over himself. He spun and tumbled in the dust, trying to right himself, and I saw at least one deformed slug come falling out of his spine, the wound closing and hiding the vertebrae again. The vampire rose to his feet, his bones cracking as he stretched himself upright with movements impossible for a mere mortal, straight into a hail of gunfire. Well, that might be pushing it. I had only two rounds left in the Schofield, I'd only loaded it with five, as the gun wasn't really safe under any circumstances to carry fully loaded. I done the same with my Colts most times, but when a fight was coming I'd top them off to a full six. I didn't dare risk it with the Schofield even under these circumstances, because a bullet shot down through my leg would pretty much be the end of things in this town, and whats worse I was carrying it Mexican bandito style, thrust through the middle of my belt. There're some things a fella can't afford to lose.

It was a good thing my two shots struck well, and the vampire twitched for a moment or two frozen in place, limbs shuddering in a sort of macabre dance, a big back door blown clean out of the back of his skull. He collapsed in a heap in front of me, but didn't turn to ash like the ones I'd killed earlier. Was it really possible these things could heal from that? I stamped down hard with the heel of my boot on its skull until it was flat as a dinner plate, its dark blood oozing into the dust. Just try knittin' that up buster!

"Clay! Look out!"

I spun, but before I could even look a horse kicked me and I went sprawling in the dust. Thats what I thought, anyway, until I looked up and saw two identical conquistadors striding toward me with an evil smile. After I shook my head there was only one, and I lifted the Schofield. The next thing I knew the gun was knocked away, which was just as well, since it was empty anyway, and the Spaniard was standing over me.

"Perhaps I underestimated you Mr. Wilder. You've bested two more of my children. It's a mistake I won't make again."

He favored me with an amused smile, then tossed me bodily across the street like a rag doll. I slammed into the remnants of the burned out saloon and came rolling to a stop on the charred floor.

Bright bursts of light flashed in my vision. I'd got myself a cracked skull once in Santa Fe, brawling with an hombre who'd taken it in his head to bend a steel poker over mine. This felt like that.

My wind knocked out of me, I lay there helpless on the floor. Pain radiated through every nerve and fiber, I felt like I couldn't move, even if I wanted to.

The Spaniard picked his way almost daintily through the wreckage. He stood beside and above me, looking smug.

"Any last words, Mr. Wilder? Would you like a chance to plead for your life? What do you think about your female companion? She really is quite beautiful. Do you think I should make her one of mine? It has been a long time since I've had a bride. I'm growing bored with this place though, and my strength has fully returned. You see, when a vampire is burnt as badly as I was, if he even survives, it takes years to recover his strength. His progeny also suffer from his debilitation, you see my children are not half so beautiful as they were in life, they lack the strength to hide their appearance. As for me, I feel well enough to make a strong new vampire, one who can retain her beauty. I just thought you should know that what is yours is now mine, before I end you. That is of course, unless you'd prefer to beg me not to, eh? What do you say?"

He was a real piece of work, this De la Vega. I flexed my fingers, getting ready to go for my derringer. He was faster than the others, but the durned fool was talking when he should have been killing me, and if I even got to put one slug into that smug mug of his I could die a smilin'.

"Muerete demonio!"

It was Maria, teeth clenched, eyes fierce, hair wild, appearing out of the wreckage wielding a bottle with a flaming rag stuffed in it.

She let fly, and the bottle soared through the air in an arc, her eyes gleaming in triumph, until the bottle thunked off the vampire's chest and fell to the floor, unbroken. The Vampire rolled his eyes and sighed.

"Perhaps my prospective bride is not so fond of me, after all. Oh very well, I shall kill you both. Farewell, Mr. Wilder."

De la Vega raised his sword, and I pulled my derringer. The conquistador looked down my barrel, amused.

"A final stand, mortal? Oh, alright, I'll play along."

He pulled his doublet to the side, exposing bare flesh.

"Take your shot, then perhaps this will feel more...sporting."

He smiled a cruel smile, and waited for it. Smug devil.

"Mighty decent of you," I drawled. "You know what the only problem with you is?" I asked.

"No, Mr. Wilder, please tell me, what is it you find lacking in my character?"

"You're not on fire."

His eyes went wide, and with that, I lowered the derringer and shot the flaming bottle. It burst, and De la Vega went up in flames like a stack of well seasoned kindling.

Maria and I covered our ears as an inhuman scream

pierced the air.

The ball of flame lashed out, knocking aside a section of the wall like it was pressboard, and he fled into the night. You could see him go for quite a ways. That tequila was pow'rful stuff.

CHAPTER 10

Maria scrounged the wreckage of the saloon for the few bottles as yet unbroken, stuffing rags in the top which she tore from her skirts. She tore another long strip and wrapped it around a piece of broken wood to make a torch. I reloaded my Colts and the Schofield, and replaced the spent round in the derringer. I had only two rounds left in my belt when I was done.

We stepped out into the street together, and saw we were surrounded by dark figures. An evil mist swarmed the streets, the moonlight cast an eerie glow on the scene. The monsters circled us, back and forth, hesitant to go in for the kill. Sending their maker off screaming into the night aflame had taught them caution, at least.

"Quick, back to back!" I snapped at Maria, and we huddled up that way, I with my Colts, she with a handful of the homemade firebombs, and the Schofield I thrust into her other hand.

"If we can get through this, perhaps we can take shelter in the church!" Maria whispered to me. I didn't think we'd make it that far.

The vampires grew more and more agitated, running back and forth like dogs, searching for an opening. It couldn't last forever, but I knew the moment I fired they would all come crashing in like a flood.

Then, a familiar voice called out from the shadows.

"Tarnation Clay! You put up a helluva' fuss, shore 'nuff!"

"Ike!" It was good to hear his voice, just now I realized I hadn't known what became of him after we was separated in the tunnels.

"Watch out Ike, these things mean business!"

"You're tellin' me Clay. Shoulda' warned me earlier though, 'afore you abandoned me down there."

"Whaddya' mean? I didn't abandon no one! We got torn apart when the river flooded in!"

"Yeah, and that worked out real good for you, didn't it Clay? Things always work out real good for you. Good ol' Clay, always looking out for number one. You escaped, I got washed back down the tunnels. They drained me dry, then turned me into one o' them. I got to say, it ain't half bad."

He stepped out into the pale moon's light, a bright red gleam in his eyes. His mouth and chest were covered in dark blood. Casually, he wiped some of it away, licking his fingers.

"You should join us. It'd be like old times. Its a hoot Clay! Ever' meal you ever tasted, every drink you drunk, every woman you had, there ain't nothin' like the blood. What's more, all this eternal damnation nonsense don't mean nothin' 'cause I'll live forever!"

"Glad you're adjustin' so well to things Ike, can't say you make it look temptin' though, not by a longshot."

He still looked mostly like himself, but his features were drawn and twisted a little, he just looked wrong.

"Don't be like that Clay, I'm bein' downright magnami... magnamio...I'm bein' real generous-like about all this. Tell you what, I'll turn you myself. We can drain that gal there just like a bottle of whiskey, just you'n me. Just think Clay, with these powers, we could be rich beyond our wildest dreams! Who could stop us?!"

"Ike, you never were the brightest of the bunch. You wasn't the bravest neither, or the slickest. Heck, most days, I didn't cotton to you much, but we rode together and I risked my neck for you, and you me, more'n once. For that, I can't leave you like this. Your soul's gone, or so I figure, and I'd like to think that even with the kind of man you were, you wouldn't have wanted to walk the earth till the end of days a monster, feedin' on the blood of innocent folks. So I'm going to kill you."

Ike guffawed.

"How you gonna' kill me Clay?! I'm durned near invincible! I'm faster, stronger, and tougher'n you'll ever be! Why, there's no man on earth can kill me! No one, no h-"

Ike's head fell clean off as something whistled through the air behind him. His mouth worked for a moment, his eyes wide, staring back up at his body. Both exploded in a burst of ash.

Father Cortez appeared out of the puff of smoke that had been Ike Turner, holding a curious looking weapon. An ornate sword, a stylized crucifix for a crossguard.

"Basura men make basura vampiros," Was the priest's grim comment as he joined us in the street.

The rest of the monsters were all worked up now, howling with rage and hunger as they edged closer and closer. This was goin' to be a real party.

The priest whispered as we faced off with the hell-things.

"Listen very carefully, amigo. I will distract them, I still have a few tricks up my sleeve. I wish I'd had time to prepare more, but it is enough. You must take my sister to the sanctuary, reach for a button under the altar that feels like a smooth stone, and that will open a door leading you to a secret room beyond. There you will find all you need to defeat this menace. Can you remember that?"

"Wait, Maria is your sister?" I was incredulous. They looked nothing alike.

"I know," he blushed, "hard to believe. She had a different father. She got looks, and I got brains."

Maria went off on another round of Gatling-gun Spanish, and I turned my attention back to the situation at hand.

The creatures snapped and slashed at the air as they closed in, slowly, warily. They would finish us. Cortez was wrong. I wouldn't get Maria out alive, even with his sacrifice. There were too many, they would destroy us. Maria lit the bottles with her torch.

"Just as I told you Clay, there are no happy endings." Maria said softly, her eyes both sad and grim.

They closed.

There comes a time in a man's life, a moment, if you will, when death approaches, the veneer is stripped away, and he is free not to hedge his bets any longer, not to worry about the morrow, but to live his last few moments well. And that, I believe, is when the flame burns hottest, brightest, just before it is snuffed out for good.

I leapt into action, about to embark on the most desperate plan of my life. There was no way it could actually work, so I grabbed Maria and kissed her deeply, taking that instant to snatch all three bottles out of her hand. I tossed them up in three different directions, and began snapping off shots. And in that moment, time ceased to exist.

I drew the bead down onto the falling bottle and sent the hammer home. As the gun bucked and flaming liquid spewed out over the monsters, I was already turning to the second bottle. I thrust the Colt up and fired, and whirled to the last bottle, falling fast, at nearly eye level with a vampire charging forward to bat it out of the way. My eyes locked with his own, burning red. I fired.

The bottle burst and the monster was engulfed in flame. Two more went down with him, tossing themselves about in the dust to try and extinguish the flames. It was no use, they seemed to burn from the inside out, and were consumed so rapidly I didn't even have time for a shot to speed them on their way. I turned again to see Father Cortez with his sword through one of the vampires guts, it was pulling itself forward along the blade to get at the terrified priest. You could almost see the memories flooding behind his eyes. I'd missed the second bottle, and now the priest was locked in mortal combat with the stuff of nightmares.

Two more of the skewered vampire's brood-mates charged, and I lit them up with both Colts at near point blank range. It seemed a'mighty hard to kill them that way, but they felt pain and I was rewarded with the very screams of the damned as they tumbled in the dust clutching and scrabbling at their wounds.

At that moment I noticed a rolled cigarette in my shirt pocket, must've forgotten it. It's funny the things your mind notices at the most inappropriate of times. I thought I'd have myself one o' them experiments, so I struck a match and lit my smoke.

Taking a puff, I dropped my match on the nearest vampire, already sweating out the soft lead slugs in torrents of blood. He burst into flames, confirming my hypo...confirming what I done guessed.

Maria came running up and booted the burning vampire into the other, and they both were reduced to ash in a matter of seconds.

I remembered Father Cortez.

He and his impaled vampire were spinning 'round and 'round, the vampire pulling himself forward on the sword, Cortez trying to hang on to it and at the same time attemptin' to keep a few feet of moonlight between him and the struggling monster.

"Hey!" I shouted to the last monster, and balled up a fist and slugged him right in his grayish, wrinkled nose.

He brought his head around again with a roar that pinned my ears back, and I scooped up the unbroken bottle and jammed it between his ragged teeth. It was quite a drink so I followed up with a lead chaser, and he too, went up in flames, leaving only a greasy dark stain on the blade of the sword.

"You ok Padre?" I puffed, taking a well deserved drag off the cigarette.

The air smelled like smoke, fire, and brimstone, and I suddenly found the main street of Rio de Sangre very unappealing.

"Don't just stand there, idiotas! Lets go!" Maria snapped

at us, so I slapped the priest on the shoulder and that seemed to wake him out of his stupor, he'd just stood there staring at the blade a while. We ran up the street and into the church.

We made the steps, and I collapsed into the first pew. The wound through my calf was starting to hurt like the blazes, and I kicked off the boot and leaned back, puffing my smoke.

"Well, that was a durn' sight o' work for one day. Give me a moment, and I'll be collecting my treasure and on my way. Nice little town y'all got here."

For all my hurts, I was in a good mood. Evil vanquished, enemies thwarted, treasure vouchsafed. I was awful tore up about losing compatriots I'd rode with for years, but I was hardened enough in my ways to think I could spend their shares of the gold at a few wild towns I knew of north of the border to ease my sorrows.

"Clay, this is not over with."

I craned my neck around. The priest looked grim.

"What! How much more can a man take?"

Maria passed by me, stuffing a few more bottles with rags to make more firebombs. I grabbed one of them from her and tore the rag out of it, gulped a goodly portion down, and splashed some on my reopened wound. It stung worser than the fires o' Hades, and I took another gulp. The burning in my throat from the caustic liquor was a welcome distraction from the stinging wound.

Father Cortez cleared his throat.

"De la Vega is indeed the vampiro from my past. He will not be so easily killed. He is very old, and he has already survived being set aflame the last time, I cannot think he will be dead this time. Also, there is no telling how many more of his kind yet infest the tunnels below. We have to finish this, before he has a chance to regain his strength and exact his revenge!"

I sighed, and took another deep drink.

"Look, I done killed who knows how many o' those critters," I began, but with a very unsubtle hmmph! from Maria amended my statement, "with Maria's help, alright? Anyways you cut it, we done killed a whole passel of monsters, and you still want me to help you go back into this fight?"

"No, senor, this is all my fault, and therefore my fight. I cannot ask you to stay if you are unwilling. I have no right. My only request, is please, take my sister to safety with you. It may be I will hold them off long enough for you to escape.

Maria punched him in the arm, to show him what she thought of his plan, then crossed her arms and glared at me.

A sudden clatter of feet and voices ascended the steps of the church.

"Oh thank God! Father! Are we saved?!"

People, families, came streaming through the door and into the church en masse. They had been hiding, terrified, while the vampires outside extracted their vengeance from house to house. A few devastated families claimed that some had even been carried off into the caverns below. Father Cortez could barely calm them down enough to make sense of it all.

Some thought the crazy gringo had killed all the vampiros, and then some were convinced the priest should perform last rites in absentia, in hopes of saving the souls of family members who had been carried off, others thought this would be a good time to make a run for it. I could only catch a bit of it here and there.

People were missing. Innocent, simple townsfolk were scared. Maria glared at me and refused to speak to me. She was convinced I was leaving. For that matter, so was I. I'd done my part, hadn't I?

It was time for these people to fight back on their own, to take control of their destiny, or some such thing. But then I watched shattered families wailing over their son or daughter that had been taken, watched the priest try to console them all, the way the terrified men of the village crowded around the doorway with pitchforks and the odd rusty rifle, desperate to protect their families yet with doom and resignation in their eyes.

Maria caught me looking at her standing there, proud and defiant, pistol in one hand, firebomb in the other. She made a point of looking away and crossing her arms again. I hung my head.

I was about to do something really, really stupid. Estupido.

Chapter 11

"What is all this stuff?" I stared about in amazement at the dusty scrolls and parchments lining the walls. A veritable library of ancient lore having to do with the eternal battle against evil lined the shelves, or so Father Cortez informed me.

What really drew my attention was a display in the corner, where an old suit of armor was posed on a stand, weapons in racks around it. There were some old rifles, a spiked head mace, and various other implements of war from a bygone era. I couldn't conjure up in my head any reason for the priest to have all this stuff.

"What's all that for," I asked, pointing. Miguel stopped trying to read something to me in Latin and looked over.

I swung the mace around in the air. "What's a priest need with stuff like this anyway? Yeah, I know, you've got some secret kind of popish thing goin' on, but hey fella' its the 19th century! We've got weapons that fire multiple times, and take less than a minute to load up. Couldn't you have had a Gatling gun or some such thing?"

"No, you must understand, the creatures are very resistant to bullets. You saw that yourself. Some of these weapons are very old, others are even sacred relics. There are those of us who believe weapons that spend long use in vanquishing the unholy can absorb a bit of that great struggle inside themselves, even be more effective against the undead, and other creatures..."

"Yeah, yeah, hey, so what's the skinny on that sword you were carrying?"

"This sword," he began, lifting it off the stand where

he'd laid it after wiping it down carefully with a white silk cloth, "Is all that is left to me of my father's memory. This is the sword I found, rusted and abandoned, and the same that saved my life, and I once believed, sent Juan Antonio de la Vega back to hell where he belongs. I was wrong, but nonetheless this sword is very unique. It has fought evil for centuries, but was considered lost when the Spanish delegation of my order disappeared after being sent to arrest Cortez and his lieutenants. It was not seen again until I discovered it in that cave. It has seen horrors undreamed of by any man alive. It has been wielded by many of the church's warriors throughout history. And now it is your turn senor. Will you wield it for God?"

Now I needed all the points I could get in that category, but in truth I was only stickin' around 'cause I just couldn't bring myself to do anything else. A needling thought somewhere at the back of my head just wouldn't shut up about findin' the nearest horse and just ridin', with a sack full of gold and as much wind as I could put behind me and Rio de Sangre. Besides, I'd heard Alaska was nice this time o' year.

It was no use, I just couldn't bring myself to light a shuck outta here like some coyote on the dodge. Besides, I told myself, there was a pile of gold with my name on it needin' liberatin' from the stables, and for that I needed a wagon, and a wagon wasn't gettin' me out of here fast enough to avoid bein' chased down in the desert by those things.

"Hey what's that?" I asked. An ornate box lay back behind a stack of books on the shelf. There was a curious engraving on the side.

"That? Oh, I don't use it."

"Why not? What's in there?"

"One of our most sacred treasures. My brothers committed it to me for just a situation such as this. But I will never be able to use it..."

"Whats the matter Padre? You ain't said enough prayers or something? What's in there anyway that certain fellas just can't use? Is it a weapon?"

"Oh it most certainly is a weapon. Here, take a look."

The Padre cleared the books off the shelf for me and motioned me forward, but seemed loath to touch the box. Was it dangerous? He sure didn't seem to want to touch it. Hell with it. I grabbed the box and opened it. My jaw nearly fell in the box, it was hanging so low.

An 1851 Navy Colt laid in the box, though it was near unrecognizable. It was deeply inlaid with Latin inscriptions and a pair of crucifixes adorned the handguards with another larger one affixed to the underside of the pommel. I'd seen most crucifixes lookin' like the good Lord was having a right good time of it, plumb comfortable up there on that cross. I didn't figure such was the case, but maybe it was just 'cause I was rarely in attendance when this kind of thing was explained. No, these crucifixes were terrible to behold. The body on them looked wretched, torn, and suffering. I swallowed a bit in my throat, so arresting was the image. That someone, no, that God His'self would do such a thing for me was something I could hardly fathom. I was a wretched vagabond, killin' and stealin' my way through life. Surely he didn't do such a thing on my account. Did he?

I took the revolver in my hand, and felt strangely affected just by holding it. I felt something come over me, some powerful urge to do something...righteous. I quickly put it down.

"That was designed by a member of our order, who used that very same pistol in the service of God decades ago. He was quite famous for it there, even if the version of the story was somewhat...sanitized to conceal certain things about the incident. He made a few modifications to it, and to my knowledge it has been used during a few...incidents, at times of the church's direst need. It was used by a young seminarian in Italy, called Possenti, who according to the official version drove off a band of soldiers with it, saving an entire town from rape and plunder."

"And what really happened?"

The priest just smiled and shut the box. He might trust me, but that didn't mean he was going to share all his secrets.

"Ok Padre, but why can't you use it?"

The priest looked abashed, a sudden color flushed his tanned cheeks.

"I cannot use this gun, nor any other. When the rifle', the gun in the old mission, exploded on me, it not only marked my face, it also scarred my mind. I have not since, and cannot ever, use another gun. I know, the same gun that injured me also saved my life. But I now suffer from a fear of them. So ashamed was I at this I could not tell my brothers when I was sent on this holy mission. In the end I just packed the gun away and said nothing. Oh, I have tried, several times. But I can barely bring myself to handle a gun, and I have never been able to pull a trigger since. I simply cannot, sudden terror overwhelms me, and I start shaking."

Indeed, his hands were shaking even now, just at the memory of it. Even if he could do it, probably wouldn't hit much, hands fluttering about like that.

"Alright, so what's with that crazy suit of armor? You ever use that?"

"Often, amigo, as you have seen, the forces of evil are not able to be defeated by mere bullets. Many times older, simpler methods must be used, beheadings, silver, piercing the heart, piles of salt, such methods require a mortal to get quite close to his target. It all depends on what one is fighting. The same methods of defense that worked well for the knights of Europe work well today."

"Wait. Piles of...salt?" "Don't ask," he said, suppressing a shudder, "It may be necessary for you to-", he began, eyeballing the suit of armor.

"Don't," I interrupted, "don't even think about it."

"But senor, it will protect-"

"Padre! Vamonos! Come quickly! They have taken

her!" "Who?!" we both turned and shouted at the same time.

An injured man stood at the door to the "secret" armory. He held a hand to his side to stanch the flow of blood from one of his wounds. He was dressed in simple peasant garb, and carried what looked like used to be a pitchfork, but the end was snapped off leaving jagged splinters of wood. There was dark blood on it.

"Your sister!" he panted. "We tried but...Maria...she was taken. We went out to try and find one of the families who had not showed up yet. We found their house, but they were all slaughtered. Then the monsters appeared, out of no-where! We were caught by suprise, it all happened so fast!"

The priest, suddenly enraged, crossed the room and lifted the man in the air by his shirt, heedless of his wounds.

"You took my sister out there?!"

The peasant grimaced, speaking quickly, "It wasn't my fault, Father! It was just going to be a few men, but your sister..."

"My sister WHAT? TELL ME?" The priest roared. I could now see the older brother who had been so protective of his family.

"Your sister...she can...," the smaller man shrugged, which looked like it hurt, "She can be very...insistent."

That was true. The priest dropped the man and collapsed against the wall, a hand over his face. The smaller man picked himself up and limped off to nurse his wounds.

"Do I abandon these people? To go and search for my sister? What if they come back?"

"Its your sister Padre, we'll get her back. You stay here with these people, I've got an idea or two," I told him, eye-ing the suit of armor.

I'd do it. I scratched my head like I was trying to get the stupid out, but it wasn't working. All for a little Spanish beauty what stole my heart like I stole gold. But I'd do it. I'd march into hell itself to save that gal, I knew right then, and not vampires nor the sense God gave a donkey would

keep me from it.
    Blast it all to hell. I'd do it.

CHAPTER 12

I felt like a durned fool. What was worse, I was right.

The armor clanked as I shuffled around in front of the entrance to the caverns. From what the townsfolk told me, there were plenty of other entrances, but she was gone and I'd rather use a tunnel I'd been down once, cause I planned on coming back in a hurry, if I made it out at all, and I can't say I was real optimistic about that.

A feller's got to have his illusions, and the suit of armor sure made a man feel a mite safer, the durn thing felt like it could stop a shotgun blast, though I wouldn't volunteer to try it.

The townsfolk had been loath to leave the sanctuary at all, even less so after the failed rescue attempt that left Maria dragged down somewhere into the inky darkness below.

I felt like I could scarce breath with the helmet on, and the visor barely allowed me to see at all, even less so in the dark, so I'd left it behind. I still wore the steel gorget around my neck though, tied on extra tight.

Across my hips I wore my guns, loaded full up with six each, my derringer thrust through the belt, along with the sword Father Cortez entrusted to me, and the holy cap and ball pistol to boot. It'd been loaded with extreme care I was told, and though I wanted to fire it off and redo the job, the priest insisted it was not a weapon to be fired lightly, and eventually I relented. That pistol gave me a wierd feeling and all, but it was still only five shots of .36 caliber, and I didn't have much faith it was going to make a heck of a lot of difference. Rounding out the walking arsenal I'd become was a double barrel shotgun to which the priest had strapped both a crucifix taken from the wall and I'd added a touch of my own. A bowie knife tied on hard with leather thongs. If I'd had time, there's lots I'd have added on still, but I already weighed myself down more than I would a horse, and time was a wastin'.

Somewhere deep in the earth below there was a gal what stole my heart somewhere between tryin' to kill me and savin' my hide. She was waitin on me now, her knight in rickety armor, coming to save her from the monsters from the pit of hell itself. For the thousandth time I felt a fool, but at least it was starting to bother me less. It was awful hard for a body to take himself serious-like while wearing a getup like that.

I shoved all other thoughts to the side. It was time to go down into that dark hole, and give the devil what 'fer.

The wind blew strong and warm, rustling the clothes of those standing around to see me off on my suicidal venture. Something tumbled along the street, coming to rest at my feet. My lucky hat. It was beat up and sweat stained, covered in dust and likely a bit of blood, and I picked it up and set it on my head. If there's such a thing as signs, I took this for a good one, and I set forth like one o' them knights of old, a'creakin' and a'clankin' on down into the wreckage of the saloon, and the darkness below.

The torch's light seemed to be swallowed up in darkness as soon as I entered the narrow passage. Down I went, keeping quiet as a man wearing a tin-can can, pausing every once in a while to listen for that ominous whooshing sound of a vampire moving at great speed, or even so much as a telltale whisper that there was something in the darkness beyond. It was cold and clammy, but I broke out in a sweat almost immediately. Whether it was from the weight of the suffocating armor or somethin' else was anybody's guess.

Father Cortez had stayed above, to protect and guide his flock in the likely event I failed my mission. I could see the vexation on his face, but he had duties to the townsfolk, and though I didn't say it, I didn't want to drag anyone else down with me to this tomb of the undead.

For a moment I'd wondered about just sending a few barrels of that dynamite off tumbling down the tunnels with a long fuse, but that would mean trapping Maria and the other prisoners down there as well, if not crushing them outright. I'd hedged my bets though, and told the Padre my plan, if'n I didn't make it back in before dawn, he was to tumble a few of the barrels and boxes down there and set them off. I grinned. At least I'd take the devils with me.

Down I went, and before long I'd reached the large hallway at the end of the tunnel, where Tanner and Hank had been sent to meet their maker. I hoped saint Peter'd been in a right good mood that day, cause those fellas' sure had some 'splainin' to do about a few nights we spent in Dodge City.

There was no way of knowing which door I should take. The floor was awful damp, probably some of the water from the underground river I'd busted into had flowed through the tunnels into this room before the river had lowered.

Listening at each door didn't help much. They way vampires had appeared at one door and then the other the last time meant they must come together somewhere in the convoluted tangle of tunnels through the rock.

I hitched up my belt and took a deep breath, and entered the door closest to me.

Time seemed to get as lost as I was in the darkness. The tunnel stretched on and on, although my keyed up nerves didn't help any. I was as high strung as a young stallion when the mares come into heat, 'ceptin' I had no expectations of a good time ahead.

At last the tunnel widened, then opened up into some kind of rough hewn chamber. There were the same kind of crude carvings in the rock the priest had described, and they looked even more primitive than the one I'd seen in the main hall.

I was driven back by a sudden wave of nausea. A stench filled the room that'd knock a buzzard off a gut truck. The odor of rotting flesh was pervasive, and waving the torch around some showed me bodies in various states of decay. Some looked dried and dusty and old, wearing grimy but ornate pieces of armor here and there, and some others were clothed as any wandering desperado, some with guns still clutched in lifeless fingers. The fresher corpses showed obvious signs of mutilation, their throats torn out, some were ripped clean in two, the torso and legs dumped atop each other. I suppressed a shudder, it was a ghastly scene. If I failed, this might be where I'd end up.

All in all though, I was somewhat heartened, even in the midst of that frightful place. There was no sign of Maria.

And then I saw it. In the wild shadows cast by the torch, a figure straightened slowly up; by the way it moved I could tell it wasn't human. My blood ran cold. I turned, just as the vampire leapt for my throat. It had been feeding on the leavings of a fresh corpse, the blood staining its jaws, almost glowing red in the light of the torch.

I dodged to the side, swinging the torch. The vampire drew up short, leaping back out of reach of the flame. It circled, hissing its anger at me through jagged teeth. The thing was even more twisted and misshapen than the ones I'd seen above ground, perhaps some half-failed child of De la Vega, cast aside to draw his unholy nourishment from the leavings of the others. Wretched and pitiful he might be, but he was still dangerous.

I didn't dare fire. If the vampires didn't already know I was here, then I'd best keep it that way for as long as I could. I drew the sword.

The vampire hissed and gurgled out a challenge, and sprang forward, despite the flame. Perhaps the thought of fresh, pumping blood was more than he could bear.

We met in the middle of the room. It swung it's gnarled claws, I my Spanish sword. Mine was sharper.

His arm dropped to the floor, the hand twitching and writhing among the lifeless limbs strewn about. The creature shrank back, clutching his wound.

"Where you goin' friend? We're just getting started here!" I taunted it, cutting off its retreat. Chance had put me between him and the door, this one didn't look to be so fast as the others. He snarled in frustration, baring his teeth in an attempt to frighten me off. I'd already seen that trick, a time or two.

I closed in.

"You and me friend, just you and me," I growled, slashing the air, driving him back against the wall. He was trapped, wounded, and scared. It felt good to be on the other side of that there equation.

I slashed out with the sword, lopping off a chunk of flesh from his shoulder. The creature screamed. I smiled.

"You and me, friend, we're gonna' get to know each other, real intimate-like." I waded in with the blade.

And there was fear in my victim's red eyes.

I was getting pretty good at this.

CHAPTER 13

It was bloody murder wipin' the blade clean of the thick dark goo coating the steel. I could only hope the long tunnels had drowned out the sounds of the struggle. All in all, I could scarce believe I made it this far without incident, though I had a ways and more to go to rescue my lady fair.

The armor was heavy. Just moseyin' around in it was like splittin' cords o' firewood. It probably didn't help that I was a tad bowlegged, neither. Those knights of old must've been some strappin' folks. Must've been quite a sight, in my steel suit o' clothes and armed to the teeth. I carefully replaced the sword in its scabbard and picked up the shotgun. Time was a wastin'.

There was only one door out of this hall of bones. I took it, holding the shotgun high with its attached crucifix ahead of me like a shield, the torch held out and high. Suddenly, I was in a great underground cavern, the stalactites hung low from heights well out of the torch's reach, water dripped and echoed through the massive chamber. I couldn't have told you north or south to save my skin.

A low growl came from somewhere in the darkness! With the echoes, it was durn near impossible to tell where it came from, I turned in wary circles, ready for attack from any direction. The way sound bounced off the walls, it seemed like I was surrounded by growling dogs straight from hell.

The vampires stepped forward in the circle of flickering torchlight.

That explained the echoes. They snapped and hissed as they approached. When a body is surrounded, it kind of simplifies things. The only thing to do is attack in all directions at once. I said simple, not easy.

I spun on a heel, leveled the shotgun and fired, blowing one's head clean off. Before his body fell apart in a pile of burning ashes, I whirled again and put the second round straight in his opposite numbers neck. This was gonna' be quite the square dance!

I pivoted to the side, and hefted the shotgun up, and the creature in front of me now recoiled suddenly at the sight of the cross, and I waved the torch around to keep them at bay. Turns out it can be mighty hard for a body to reload a shotgun while keeping it upright and swinging a torch at the same time. I'd just fingered a few shells out of the bandolier when something struck me in the back hard enough to kill me, if'n I wasn't covered in hard steel. I tumbled forward, losing the torch and the shotgun in the process.

I craned my head around to get an upside down view of three pairs of glowing red eyes a'charging me, and managed to leverage myself upright in the heavy armor just in time to go down in a pile of clutching, clawing hellbeasts. The misshapen creatures roared and snapped at each other as each tried to go for my throat at the same time. My arms were pretty well pinned, but I wasn't having none of that. I ducked my head, narrowly avoiding the snap of powerful jaws, then butted up hard with my noggin right into a snarling face. The snarl turned into a shriek, and I lifted my knee into the next creature. We were all in a tangle, and strong as they were, none of us had any leverage.

We fell down again, and I lashed out with a steel-clad elbow, smashing a few of one's teeth in the process. Something struck a glancing blow against my head that like to have killed me if it'd landed proper.

I craned one arm around, struggling with all my might to catch hold of somethin' tender. Their arms were trapped beneath me. In the bare light of the fallen torch I could barely see anything but the reflected light in their red eyes.

One vamp opened his jaws wide and clamped down on my throat. His teeth shattered against the steel. I caught hold of something on the other critter's face, dug my fingers in, and pulled. The critter gave a sharp wail and gnashed his teeth, I could still feel my fingers, so I guessed I hadn't been tugging at the monsters mouth. I tugged for all I was worth, and finally something gave way, tearing clean up and off. The monster pushed away from me, tumbling the other off my neck and I tossed its nose to the side, climbing heavily to my feet. I sprang for the shotgun, and the vamp what still had his honker charged me. I whipped the shotgun up over my shoulder and stepped to the side, and used all my weight and strength to bring it back around. Whap!

The monster was caught up short, his flattened skull slammed back into the rock as his heels went to the sky. The last monster caught me blindside as I stood there admirin' my handiwork like a fool. We tumbled back, my steel suit scraping loudly against the rocks with a sound that made me want to tear my ears off.

The creature was atop me, bellowing down into my face. His breath made me wish I'd torn my own nose off. If I survived the night I resolved to put my eyes out as well. The vampire-beast was bein' plumb unsociable, so I rapped him one with my free hand and stretched the other out towards the fallen torch. Just a few inches too far!

Those mighty jaws lunged down at me, and I managed to get my arm in between them and me just in time. The creature beared down on me, I pushed back at him. I was quickly losing this battle of strength. The slavering jaws edged closer and closer. I fair dislocated my shoulder doing it, but finally my fingers brushed the torch. I dug my nails in, dragging it to my hand. The jaws enveloped my head, coating my face in foul saliva.

I slammed the torch into the creature's ear. He screamed so loud I figured my eardrums was pierced for sure, but the beast's head caught fire and we rolled over and over, the vampire still scrabbling and clingin' to my armor, me shouting and clawing for all I was worth to get away from the thing. He was trying to take me with him.

I used a stalagmite to pull myself to my feet, slashing back with elbow after elbow in a desperate attempt to free myself from the burning vamp. My armor conducted the heat right into the suit, my skin scalding as I tried to shrink up inside the armor. It was hot as hellfire of a sudden, and I turned and slammed the creature up against the rock pillar, trying desperately to get him off. He scrambled around to the front, tearing at the steel with his claws. If I hadn't worn the armor I'd be shredded meat right about now. I struck out hard and then grabbed hold of the creature, if I didn't knock him loose soon, this devilish rodeo would be the end of me as well. Now, let me tell you, this bull can buck!

I wrapped my arms around the struggling vampire, and drove my legs forward. I was falling as much as I was running, but I kept my legs a pumping, the skin stretching tight across my face from the heat. My eyes shut tight, I drove forward with every last ounce of strength in my body.

We slammed into the wall. The vampire burst apart, black grease and sizzling ash filled the air around me, flooding my lungs.

The wall gave way, and I tumbled into light.

CHAPTER 14

My lungs ached from the burning air, my stomach roiled from the stench of brimstone. I alternated between coughing up black smoke and retching thick bile over my boots.

I kicked the last of the smoldering remnants off my boot and let my eyes adjust to the light.

"Nice of you to join us, Mr. Wilder."

Aw, shucks.

The undead conquistador sat a carefully wrought stone chair, the room lit by sconces filled with brightly burning candelabras. The Vampire wore fresh clothes, aged and yellowed lacy collar and cuffs, silk doublet in yellow and red. He had been badly affected by the burning, but even through his blackened skin I could make out the scowl on his face. This feller didn't seem quite so pleased to see me.

"I see you've been even further reducing my numbers Mr. Wilder. I congratulate you on your success. My children are dear to me, though the ones you killed were made when I was recovering from a wounded condition even deeper than you see me now. But despite this (He brushed off a few flakes of burnt skin from the back of his hand) I am still quite strong, and the time has come for me to leave this place, and set forth with a new army, to conquer this territory yet again. You merely hurried things along. I half expected you to run like a scalded dog. I couldn't allow that. In your arrogance, I wagered you would leave all hope of safety or escape, and come right to my waiting arms. Fortune provided me with the ransom I needed to ensure your arrival. Is this how men of your century protect your women?"

De la Vega let out a soft chuckle.

"If so, all the better for me to unleash my dark army upon the world, and return things to their proper place. From what I understand, things above are quite a mess, so different from my time. Your rulers are chosen amongst yourselves, and with predictable results. The people while away their time in idle pursuits, when they could be producing so much more! Your buildings lack the beauty of those of my time, built for petty function, not to stun the ages with their magnificence! The people to the north, your people, roam carelessly to and fro, searching for land and gold, violence and lawlessness the only rule.

This will change! I will sweep forth with my armies, turning those few worthies to my cause, to create a dark empire such as the world has never seen! The rest of worthless humanity will be brought to heel under my tread, those unwilling to be forced to greatness shall be harvested as cattle!"

He slumped back in his chair, suddenly slack, as if the fire had gone out of him. I darted my eyes down to my guns and sword, making sure they were in their proper place. There was at least one fella in this room in dire need of their attention.

"But this is all exhausting. You managed to weaken me with your little fire, I'll grant you that much. But I will heal soon, nourished by the blood of those ignorant peasants you feel bound to protect. We will drain this town dry, and burn the remains. Then we march west and north, rallying the worthy to our cause."

"What makes you think people will support the wholesale slaughter of their kind? Why tell me all this anyway?"

"I tell you this because I will be killing you, very soon. I want you to know what will become of your world. I want you to know the suffering you have brought to the people of this town, who will be harvested well before their time. If not for your arrival, it might have been years before I felt compelled to sally forth on my great mission. No matter, it would happen sooner or later. Mankind will forever fall on their knees before the strong, before those they might worship here on earth, before leaders who can promise them a brighter future. I was born to conquer, as a mortal, and now, even more so, a dark lord, bringing order and rule to the chaos of this age. The Aztecs never knew what they had, twisted creatures dwelling in the depths of their mud and stone structures, deliberately kept weakened, fed human sacrifices on their holy days, worshipping the creatures of darkness as "gods", when they could have declared war on God Himself!"

De la Vega's words echoed through the great room.

He'd worked himself up again, and collapsed back into his chair with a sigh.

"But enough of this. It is time that you died. You are a most fitting first victim of this revolucion'! Everything you stand for I stand against. Your unsavory dress, your brash manner, your disrespect of your elders and betters. It will be a pleasure to wipe the memory of you from the face of the earth. Meet the first of my new army!"

He waved his hand with a flourish, and from an opening behind the throne came ten of the local villagers. They were obviously turned.

They weren't the mangled, twisted and demonic creatures I'd seen before, you could just barely tell they were no longer human. Their vacant smiles exposed neat, sharp fangs, their eyes burned with hunger. They knelt in reverence and fealty to their new lord.

"These newborn children of mine have committed their immortality to my service, the new life I have granted them in exchange for their undying fealty. You see how they obey? There were a few too stubborn to appreciate what I offered, who clung to their foolish crosses, even when I tore the life from their bodies. It only took an example or two to make them see the wisdom of submitting to their new ruler. They are faster, stronger than my previous children. But I digress. I have spent many a night on my throne, nothing but my own thoughts to entertain me. I am in the mood for some festivities, before my feast. There's nothing quite like a performance before supper. Watching a man ripped limb from bloody limb. I'm already getting hungry, just at the thought of it. Tell me, does it trouble you that I will soon suck the bleeding marrow from your bones? That your life's blood will further my own existence? That your death will be my cure? "

He was a real snake, this one. Even in his blackened and weakened condition, his eyes burned brightly as he taunted me about my impending death. That same glint was in the smiling eyes of his new "army", poor peasants who'd exchanged their souls for unlife, if it bought them even an hour more upon the earth. There was nothing of their former selves left. Their souls were gone, they were mere animated shells, consumed by evil.

My fingers itched, I steeled myself to draw. If I had one last act upon this earth, I would put as many slugs as I could into this arch-fiend. In his weakened condition, maybe, just maybe, it would be enough to kill him. But any and every drop of suffering I could wring out of him would be payment enough for centuries in hell.

"And now," he clapped once, "Let the dance begin!"

As one, the new vampires bared their fangs with a hiss.

My guns cleared leather, and I blazed away with both barrels.

Almost instantly, the assembled vampires zipped into the path of the bullets, their sharp white teeth glinting in the candlelight. They stood in the path of the gunfire, soaking it up without complaint. Stronger indeed. Before I could react, my hands were seized and stretched wide by fingers of stone. A vampire stood at each side, tugging my arms apart until my feel left the ground.

I struggled, but it was like trying to pull the earth and sky together. Neither end budged. The other vampires took

step after step closer to me. It was over. I closed my eyes.
Maria, forgive me.

CHAPTER 15

The conquistador laughed with unrestrained glee.

"Stop!" He commanded, and the vampires backed away, save the ones holding me.

"Once again, quite disappointing Mr. Wilder. I was just beginning to think there was something special about you after all. Oh, never mind. On to the next course, shall we? I'm positively famished!"

"Get this over with De la Vega! You've got me, now finish this already! What more could you possibly want with me?!" I snarled, baring my teeth uselessly. I was trapped like a rat in...yeah.

"Why, I want your suffering, of course. And I've saved the best part for last!" The old vampire sat back in his stone chair, quite pleased with himself. He snapped his fingers, and two new vampires dressed as attendants came forth, holding someone in a torn and tattered dress, struggling like a wildcat. There was a hood over her head, concealing her face, but there was only one woman I knew who could put up a fight like that.

De la Vega rose, and removed the hood with a flourish. Maria cursed and spat at him for a moment, then she saw me.

"Clay!" She struggled vainly against the vampires holding her.

"Maria!" I shouted back.

"What are you doing here! Of all the stupid things..."

"It wasn't my first choice of ways to while away the evening, believe me. But when I'd heard you'd been taken-"

"Wait...you came to rescue me? Is that...armor you are wearing"

Despite the danger, I flushed with embarrassment. I was feeling a'mighty sheepish about now, especially so with Maria's eyes boring into me like that. There was something strange about that look too, but I couldn't quite put my finger on it. It looked like-"

"How utterly delightful," the vampire clapped his hands and cackled. He needed suffering and pain more than he needed blood, and he needed killin', and right bad at that.

"My dear," De la Vega began, tracing a blackened finger over Maria's cheek, leaving a trail of soot, "I have been waiting for this moment for a long time."

"Bastardo!" Maria spat at the ground, jerking away as much as she could, held firmly in place by her captors.

"Now, now, my dear, is that any way to talk to your lord husband?"

Maria was the very spirit of defiance. "Never! There is nothing you could do to make me marry a monster like you! El diablo!"

"Are you sure? Oh, very well then." He gestured languidly to the vampires holding me stretched tight in the air. If it weren't for the tightly laced armor, my shoulders would have been ripped from their sockets. "Kill him," the vampire commanded with exaggerated indifference. I'd no notion I'd be getting off that easy.

"Stop! Wait!" Maria screamed, and the vampire played his part. He turned back to Maria, as if an afterthought.

That gal looked me in the eye, even from across the room, her eyes filled mine bigger than the sun.

"Maria, don't! Aaaaack!" I was cut short by a sudden tug from each side. I was pretty sure one shoulder was out of joint. The pain brought tears to my eyes. At least, I thought it was the pain what done it, and I steeled myself for what would come next.

She turned from me after a longing look. Her eyes lowered, she nodded.

"I will do it. Just...don't hurt him," She turned to the

conquistador, "Don't hurt Clay."

The vampire nodded, solemnly. He approached her, slowly, almost tenderly, taking her face in his burnt hands, tilted her head back, and struck.

"NOOOOOOOOOOOOooooooo!" I cried, my soul felt like it was ripping out of my chest.

The vampire sank his teeth deep, sucking greedily at the veins of her neck, enraptured in his victory.

I'd failed. It didn't matter if I died. I would've leapt straight into hell if I could of done it to save that gal. But it was too late. Not only had she surrendered her soul to darkness, the undead bride of a monster in every sense of the word for all eternity, but she'd done it to save me.

De la Vega pulled back with great effort, his head back, his tongue running over his lips, savoring every drop. He used a fang to open up a vein on his wrist, and let a huge quantity of blood flow into her open mouth.

"That's right, drink well my child. You shall be my strongest, my best. My queen."

He let Maria fall to the floor.

She lay limp, her eyes glassy, her chest barely heaving.

"I have drained her to the point of death, but not beyond. She will rise shortly, my child, my bride, to serve me in unlife, eternally. She shall be my queen. I shall be her king. This must be hard for you, but you must take heart. She shall forget you, in time. And time is all she has now."

The vampire gloated. His laughter rose slowly until it filled the cavern. My face twisted up, my heart was shattered. I could not speak, I could only glare out my hatred at the devil who'd stolen everything from me. My gold, my life, my woman.

He waved a lazy hand and turned away.

"You may kill him now."

The pressure on my arms increased, they were going to tear me apart. The cords on my neck strained, my muscles cracked, it was all in vain against the unholy strength that would tear me asunder in mere moments.

Maria lay asprawl on the dais, reaching out to me with one hand, her eyes full of love, and sorrow. Her lips moved soundlessly then her eyes glazed over, and she was still.

I screamed my rage to the heavens. The demons cackled.

Maria's words came back to me. There are no heroes.

I was already in hell.

CHAPTER 16

My teeth gritted against the pain, I struggled with all my might against the vampire's slow, inexorable pull.

They grinned at me, their fangs gleaming in the candle-light. My other shoulder popped. I screamed, in spite of myself.

"In nominae patri, et fili, et spiritu sancti! Muerete!"

The vampires turned their heads in a flash, fangs bared, hissing.

The padre loomed tall in the doorway, his flat brimmed hat turning his eyes into pools of shadow. He held a rosary in one hand, a large glass decanter in the other.

He stepped into the great room, his arm coming around in a wide arc. The clear liquid slashed across the room in a wide stream.

The vampires holding me let go, hands scratching at their faces and arms, a great pile of steam rose from their pale skin as it began to melt almost instantly. The assembled demons tumbled to the ground, writhing in pain.

"Agua bendita! Holy water!" The priest explained, and unslung a great axe from his back. He charged into the room, hacking the heads off screeching vampires as he went.

I fell to my knees, my hands flexing, I grabbed my shins, and pulled upwards. My shoulders popped back in place, and I fell forward on my face, dizzy with pain.

My eyes shot open, my body shook, and suddenly all I could feel was a burning rage.

Ignoring the fire in my shoulders, I leapt to my feet, draw-ing my sword.

I joined the Padre, slashing and slicing away, still gnashing jaws worked soundlessly as severed heads rolled across the floor, then burst apart in a shower of cinders. The new vampires were helpless, the holy water smoked like acid on their skin.

De la Vega reappeared, snarling at me from atop the dais. He charged, not so fast as the first time we'd met, but he was still a blur. My breastplate folded under his fist, and I went tumbling back to the far wall. On the way into this cursed town, I seen a small boy kickin' a tin can down the road. This must've looked something like that. I hit the wall hard and fell flat on my face. I couldn't breathe.

Next thing I knew, I was seized by the throat and slammed against the wall. I looked down into the enraged red eyes framed in the scorched flesh of De la Vega's face.

"You FOOL!" he boomed, and his voice seemed to shake the very walls.

His grip on my throat was so tight I couldn't speak, so in reply I clenched my fist and slugged him right across his burnt, ugly, face.

Some charred flesh tore free and he howled in fresh rage and pain, but before I could so much as try and work free of his grasp he slammed me up against the wall again, a flash of light burst in my skull.

"You DARE challenge me, MORTAL?!" two hideous faces screamed at me. I aimed for the middle one and hit him again. It was a losing battle, but I'd play it out as long as I could.

A bit of his nose fell off this time, which really made him mad. He slammed me against the wall again and again, my head rapping back and forth against the stone, my breast plate getting tighter and tighter as it collapsed under the abuse. He'd crunch me up in a big tin ball if this kept up. Canned outlaw.

In between concussions, I caught a glimpse of Miguel, sprinting at us with axe raised high. Had to keep the vampire busy, or Miguel'd get cut to shreds before he could land a single blow.

I fought back as best I could, every three or four times I smacked the wall I managed to throw a half-hearted fist into the works, which didn't do much but make De la Vega slam me that much harder, chunks of stone crumbling from the wall.

Then Miguel was there, swinging the axe for all he was worth. My skull cracked the wall. The room spun. The axe fell.

And came to a sudden stop a foot from De la Vega's cussed head.

The conquistador dropped me, and I sank against the wall, still seeing double.

Except one of those doubles was holding the axe and wearin' a hat, and the other held the shaft stock still, keeping the blade from splittin' the bad guy's head clean in two.

I blinked, because they both looked the same. Only one of the doubles was a mite younger looking, with pale white skin and no scars. Miguel must've been confused too, because he looked like he done seen a ghost.

My head cleared, and so did the scene before me.

"Miguel. It has been a long time, my son." Father Cortez, senior, looked emotionless, pale and still. His tone was flat.

"Father? How could...Is it you?" Miguel's hands on the axe trembled; his father tore it easily from his grasp and tossed it carelessly across the room.

"Father! How is this possible?!" Miguel backed away, holding his head in disbelief.

"Miguel, this must be hard for you. You were so young when we were separated." The priest intoned, gliding forward smoothly toward Miguel, grasping him gently by the shoulders.

"No Father! You are one of them! How could this be?" Miguel threw his hands down in disbelief.

"My son...my son, there there. I have a new god now. The God of my fathers abandonded me when I needed him most. My lord, my new lord, showed me mercy, even for my great transgressions. He showed me the error of my ways. It was he, and not...HIM who granted me eternal life, showing me mercy I'd never dreamed of..."

"Nonono! Father, this in not you! Your soul!"

The elder Cortez interrupted with a sudden snarl.

"My soul means nothing! Miguel, what is in your soul? Does your soul tell you to follow meekly along while others grow in wealth and power, father children and legacies, enjoy the pleasures you have never known? Does your precious little soul tell you to sacrifice yourself for those weaker than you? Does your soul tell you these things? No Miguel, your soul tells you to dance in the dark night, taking what you can for yourself, punishing the weak and fearing the strong, your soul wants pleasure, and abandon, and revelry. I know this, because mine did. I spent a lifetime denying my true nature, and look what it did to us, to our family!"

The vampire-priest's anger melted away as quickly as it came, and he continued.

"But we can continue now, we can begin anew. We can spend an eternity as father and son, bound in love and service to the new lord and savior, and we can truly, this time, change the world! Join me Miguel, and say farewell to pain and sickness and silly rules made by men in silly hats, oceans away!"

Miguel looked up, sorrow flooding his eyes.

"I am sorry father. I am sorry for you, and sorry for your soul. I hoped one day to join you in the afterlife. I spent years dreaming about what I would say to you. The father I never really knew, and now never will."

Miguel's father raged, suddenly darting forward, closing the distance between father and son. Miguel backpedaled in terror, his father following, hands clenching.

"Then if you truly reject me Miguel, if you truly want to

disappoint me, I WILL DESTROY YOU!" The vampire screamed.

Miguel looked frozen with fear, more of the father he never had than the enraged vampire stalking towards him. De la Vega watched the whole scene with a smile, unable to resist feeding off the anguish of servant and son.

The moment was now. I lashed out with my fingers, tearing into the charred flesh of De La Vega's side. A big chunk tore clean off, I flung it across the room. The injured vampire stumbled away, shoving me back against the wall with a stunning backhand.

I crumpled to the floor, my ribs were probably cracked, my breathing came ragged now, slicing my ribs with every heaving breath. I grit my teeth and dug out the crucifix laden revolver.

"Miguel!" I forced out, and tossed the revolver across the room. He turned, and the revolver bounced off his chest onto the floor next to him. He looked from it to his snarling father above.

Almost gingerly, he took up the revolver.

He held it out, his hands shaking mightily. Oh brother, this wasn't looking good for either of us.

"Father, I am sorry."

"Don't whine at me, you little runt!" Screamed the vampire in priest's clothing.

"You disobey me! You dare raise a gun to your own sire!" Miguel's pappy paced back and forth, seeking an opening.

"You are not my father." Miguels voice was flat, then the gun suddenly steadied, still as steel, and he pulled the trigger.

The muzzle bucked, and the vampire was jerked plumb off his feet, as if smashed by a powerful blow. That wasn't no ordinary .36, right there.

Miguel unleashed with a fury, thumbin' back the hammer and bustin' loose with giant thundering balls of flame from the mouth of the big pistol, while the collared vamp tumbled and reeled with every blow as if smashed by a giant hammer.

The cap and ball ran dry with an ominous click.

Trembling with fury and pain, Miguel's father lurched to his feet and charged, fangs bared.

I was tryin' to scramble to my feet, but a sudden burst of pain tore through my guts and my legs went weak. I collapsed, heaving as sharp razors cinched tighter and tighter around my lungs with every breath.

"My son, my only son. YOU. ARE. NOT. MY SON!" The vampire shrieked in Miguel's face, his voice preternaturally high pitched.

He lifted Miguel high against the wall, his fangs bared for the kill.

"But you were once my father, and if you still were, I would tell you...I love you papa."

Miguel, with steady hands now, dug out one o' them bottles Maria had prepared. He struck a match on his long coat, and lit the fuse.

The vampire froze when he saw the flaming bottle of tequila, his eyes coming up to meet Miguel's.

Miguel's eyes closed. His face was peaceful.

He dropped the bottle.

It shattered on the stone, the pair were instantly engulfed in bright tongues of flame.

The vampire jerked, but Miguel closed his arms around him with desperate strength, a solitary, final embrace.

The remnant of the priest that was Father Cortez, senior flaked away in red rimmed ashes.

Miguel fell forward, collapsing to his knees, ashes scattering. He fell forward on the floor, dead. Rest in peace, Padre'.

CHAPTER 17

I wanted to kill everything left in the room. Maria had been drained almost to the point of death, sacrificing herself in an ultimately useless gesture to save my life. Soon, she would rise a vampire, a dark bride for a dark lord. There wouldn't be anything left of her. My throat tightened. There might not be much I could do but hope to die before I saw her like that. De la Vega was still clutching his torso where I'd torn off a good chunk of flesh, and I decided perhaps he was right about one thing, the suffering of your enemies does taste sweet. I charged with my sword drawn in my right hand, a Colt in my left.

The two servants left their posts beside the throne and zipped into position between me and their maker, fangs bared. I shot one through the forehead and slashed with the sword, toppling the second acolyte's head to the floor. As the first collapsed as if struck by the hand o' God His'self, I finished the job with short, brutal strokes.

The vampires had obviously been granted their positions for their extreme lack o' sense, 'cause they could have torn me up right easy had they dispensed with the threats and made with the killin'. Why does everybody talk so much?

De la Vega was next. He spun, quicker than a barn cat, and slashed at me with his bony claws. I barely dodged, moving on pure reflex, the blow whistled past my face, an inch from taking my head with it.

De la Vega roared and drew his sword in a slashing arc. I growled right back at him, charging forward, swinging the blade with abandon.

De la Vega was injured. He'd been burned and tore up

some, even if I'd gotten the short end of our little scrap. Still, he was far stronger and faster than any mortal man, and a trained swordsman to boot. He parried my blows easily, a wicked looking grin stretching the blackened skin taut, his eyes gleaming red in the candlelight.

I struck harder, faster, driven by a burning rage that threatened to consume me. I abandoned any attempt at defense and just kept bulling forward, hacking back and forth two handed with the blade.

He parried my best blows lazily, then snarled and began his counterattack. His elegant sword moved almost too fast to see, a thousand flames glittered in the flashing steel. I dodged and blocked on panicked reflex, his sword scraping against my steel armor time and again, scoring the carefully wrought steel with deep gouges.

He was toying with me, he wanted me to see my death coming, to be utterly defeated. I'd never held a sword before this one, he was trained by the flower of Spanish warriors in his time, his skills forged and hardened in the deadly battles of another age.

De la Vega caught my blade on his own, scraping the edge along mine, circled it around, and then the sword was torn from my grasp. He swung the blade in easy circles, taunting me with his arrogant smile, showing me his pearly white choppers. I'd been using the wrong tools. It was time to do this my way.

The twin Colt's cleared leather with a life of their own. De la Vega's eyes went wide, my view of them obstructed by a bead over each pupil. I thumbed back the hammers and-

They were struck away. The sudden blow knocked me to the ground.

I froze at the sight. Maria stood above me, dim red lights behind her eyes, canines sharp, pressing against her lower lip. The barest hint of a tan was still detectable on her skin, only a beauty mark marred her alabaster smoothness. All was lost.

"Maria! I-" She moved faster than they eye could follow, she was still, then suddenly she was inches from my face, a slender finger pressed against my lips. It was cold as stone. She laughed, a throaty, eerie sound.

"Shut up, Estupido Mortale. I don't want to hear your whining."

She stood, mocking me with her eyes, her hands on her hips.

"What? You thought we shared something...special?" Her lips pouted, she affected a pathetic tone.

"You fell in love, didn't you? You stupid, stupid man! You should have left when you had the chance. Before this...semental de la noche, before he bested you."

De la Vega's lips twisted cruelly. He was soaking it up. Maria went to him, her fingernails, now long and sharp, trailing lightly across his chest.

" And now, before you go the way of all men, Clay Wilder, you should be the witness to our dark union, our first kiss."

Passionately, tenderly, she brought her lips to De la Vega's scorched flesh. Her hands reached for him, bringing his face to her own.

If I'd eaten recently, it'd have been all over the armor in a heartbeat.

The worst sight of my life played out before me, the gal I'd fallen so sudden and so hard for, the gal I'd tried against all odds to save and failed, tanglin' tongues with my worst enemy. Blech!

The kiss went on and on, until I thought I might as well just have a bullet for dinner and a long nap. De la Vega spared a glance my way, just to revel in my anguish. One eye glinted at me, fierce delight evident in his triumph, and my anguish. That eye flashed wide a second later, and his hands shot out, desperately trying to pull away from his new bride.

Maria bit down even harder on his lip, shaking her head

like a dog does a rat. De la Vega began to scream, a horrible, squealing sound, and Maria ripped back, spitting what was left of his lower lip across the great stone room. It landed wetly on the cold stone floor.

De la Vega spun away, retreating, holding his face and muttering unintelligible curses. Maria stalked after him, a quiet, deadly rage behind her glowing eyes. She kicked over a wooden stand and snapped off a leg like you'd pick a flower. Grabbing De la Vega by his lacy doublet, she stretched him upright and jammed the stake through his guts. Now that's more like it!

The "Dark Lord" of the new era backpedaled, trying to tear the splintered piece of wood from his guts, and I thought it was time to lend the lady a hand. Maria swung on him, but he batted the blow aside and backhanded her across the room with a snarl. I charged, ramming my armor plated shoulder into the vampire, just as he straightened up and saw me coming. We went down in a pile, and I struck out. My fist slammed against the rock, shooting bolts of fresh pain up my arm, and De la Vega seized me by the throat, and began to squeeze. My air choked off; all I could do was batter weakly against his unholy strength. Spots swarmed in my field of view, I would black out in a few seconds. The cords in my neck flexed and strained against the crushing grip, choking the very life from me.

Another pair of hands what seemed to be made if smooth stone wrapped themselves around my neck, began prying free the deadly grip around my windpipe.

De la Vega added his other hand to the mix, my vision was growing dark. The vise tightened, I thought my neck would snap. I wasn't contributing much to this here effort; my thoughts were coming slow and thick, like syrup. My gun! All sense of distance disappeared; I reached down a mile and then some to fumble around for my revolver. My fingers brushed something rough and hard, my fingernails scratching against the stone floor. I scrabbled wildly for anything resembling the butt of my Colt as Maria grunted behind me from the effort of preventing my neck from being snapped.

My fingers found purchase, the image of De la Vega's twisted face swam before my eyes. He yelled something at me from far away and underwater. My head felt like it would pop clean off, blood pounding and throbbing through my skull. I couldn't tug the revolver free. It was caught up on something. Had...to...draw!

Maria screamed from the effort, pulling for all she was worth, which saved my neck bones but only choked me harder. My jaw went slack, my tongue rolled out. I sank back down and away, the vision from my eye sockets disappearing somewhere up above me, farther and farther away.

The world swam in flames, but all was darkness around. Was this hell? Was I dead? I thought I heard Maria screaming, long ragged cry from another world.

A dark figure sat on a dark throne atop a pyramid of dark stone. Terrified victims chanted unintelligible phrases over and over again, carried by still more dark figures to the throne, offering their throats to a dark god. The flames shot up, briefly revealing my nemesis, blonde and eternally young, smiling cruelly as victim after victim were presented for his waiting fangs. Was this a vision of the past? Or the future?

A shriek pierced my ears, it was my name being called, a female voice.

A heartbeat.

A flash of vision, staring down into a hideous face, gnashing its teeth at me.

Another beat. My vision was black, but the smooth familiar grip of the Colt filled my hand. Darkness.

Yet another heartbeat, and my thumb found the hammer, I twisted the gun in its holster around 'til the barrel jammed into something hard and crusty. A loud long BOOM from somewhere in the deep below. The grip loosened a little, a flash of white.

Hammer. Thumb. Trigger. Finger. Pull!

Again and again I repeated the process, it was all I could do to think that far. A pressure lifted, a choking breath, and I hurtled back into the saddle in my head, took the reins and wagged my head about lookin' for that thrice-cussed side-winder what needed killin'.

I was being dragged across the floor. De la Vega lay writhing in pain, shouting dire threats.

"He's too strong Clay! We have to get out of here!"

I was coughing too hard to protest, my throat felt like I'd just been punched in it, scratchy and sharp. My lungs heaved even as they threatened to turn inside out.

I aimed between my boots to take a good last shot at De la Vega, and was rewarded with a howl as the tip of his boot was nipped clean off.

"Clay, get up!" Maria shouted, hauling me to my feet like I weighed no more'n a child. I grabbed her arm as she turned toward the door, and drew her into mine. I kissed that gal for all she was worth, dippin' her back right proper like. I might not be able to beat De la Vega in a swordfight, but I was an old hand at this game, and a body has to take his victories where he can.

Maria clutched me harder than she probably intended, I was worried she would crush my already-cracked ribs. But I didn't show it. I even managed to ignore the sudden sharp pain in my mouth. Dang but those teeth were sharp!

I stood her up, and bent down to sweep my hat off the floor. Maria smoothed her dress. Maria wasn't some blood-thirsty demon from hell, a shell of who she'd been in life. If anything, those fangs just gave a proper warning of just how dangerous this petite little gal was, to your head and your heart. Neither of mine had stopped aching since the first night we met, though for different reasons. I could only guess she still was who she was because of something to do with her not makin' a willing choice. Maybe she still had her soul and all. But the villager's hadn't much of a choice either. But they'd chosen more time on this sorry earth rather than lookin' forward to the next one, and Maria had done it for me. She died...for me. She was willin' to give her soul...for me.

Maybe it was 'cause she made the greatest sacrifice one could, or maybe, just maybe, it was somethin' else, somethin' special, they say only comes along once in a century, true-

Nah. That stuff was for fairy tales.

"Quickly Clay! Vamonos! Arriba!" She urged. Though when she turned away I could swear I saw a sharp smile spread across her face.

De la Vega shouted after us, threats to destroy us all, drain us dry, the usual. I knew just how to deal with that ne'er do well, but it would have to wait until I got to the surface. We ran to the door behind the throne.

"This way may be quicker!" Maria suggested, and we swung the heavy wooden door open. We both gasped in unison.

Rows upon rows of wood coffins lined a long room, disappearing off into the darkness. There could be hundreds! The coffins were covered in heavy chains, thick crude iron padlocks clung to the sides.

I stared in amazement. There could be hundreds of bodies in there, vampires all, enough to swarm the town past all hope of defense, enough to take town after town, turning more and more as they went, like a snowball running down a mountain up Colorado way.

Blood dripped from my cuts and scrapes, a heavy droplet rolled down my fingers, and fell, a little splash of color on the dirty floor.

The coffins began to rattle and rock side to side as something terrible inside each and every one struggled to get out. Muffled cries of hunger echoed in the long chamber. The echoes went back farther and farther. De la Vega had a hole card.

"You see?!" The wounded vampire screamed from behind us. He lay on the floor where we'd left him. He was healing, his wounds knitting together, much more slowly now, but he was gathering strength. He cackled as he rolled up to a knee.

"Do you see how…HOPELESS it is to oppose me!" he screamed at us with clenched fists.

"Do you think I would even ALLOW you to foil my plans?!" He took a shaky step forward; a deformed slug pushed out from his knee to ping off the hard stone.

"Clay…we need to get out of here!" Maria whispered sharply in my ear.

I tugged my hat down tight.

"I reckon',"I began, and I suddenly lost my balance and my knees went weak. I caught myself before I fell, but the ceiling seemed to be a'rockin' back and forth some, and I felt a mite woozy.

No sooner'd I took a step towards the entrance than the little gal a'hoisted me up over her shoulder like a sack o' taters and took off at a run.

"Just hang on tight and I will carry you, my knight in shining armor."

It was plumb humiliatin', being toted about like that, but just the same I was all tuckered out, what with carryin' folks this way and that all day, engagin' in fisticuff's and sword-fights with vampires and such. Maria could be right handy to have around. What a gal!

CHAPTER 18

Maria took off at a dead run, sprinting faster than any man I ever knowed and you couldn't even tell she was carrying my weight to boot. She picked up speed as she went, till we were whippin' around corners and dodging through doorways like a sparrow flies. Maybe faster.

"Do you even know where you're going?!" I shouted over the rush of wind caused by our swift passage. I was getting a'mighty sick to my stomach, the little bit I could see was movin' pretty fast. If'n we got out o' this mess, and I could find a way to dress her up as a horse, Maria could make me a fortune at the races out Arizona way.

"I can sense the direction we need to go, but I've never been in these tunnels before! I don't know which turn to take!" She called back over her shoulder. I hung over the tiny gal, my guns drawn and ready to go fourth of July on anything that so much as twitched behind us. Didn't figure on De la Vega just lettin' us go on our way.

I wasn't disappointed. I could see the barest outline of a dark shadow come tearing around the corner behind us, glowing red eyes filled with rage. I fired. In the light of the muzzle flashes De la Vega's teeth gleamed as he let out a terrifying roar. My guns bucked and roared back, catching him here and there in his chest, a few more went wide, sparking off the walls. It slowed him a bit, but as fast as Maria ran, he kept up.

"Clay! The tunnels fork up ahead!" Maria called a warning, her vampiric eyes seeing far into the darkness beyond. I was near blind.

"Take it!" I shouted back, being a bit busy at the time. I

snapped off my last two shots, one caught the pursuing vampire in the knee, and he tumbled, bouncing this way and that off the walls in a shower of splintered stone. Ought to slow him down a bit.

The tunnel angled upwards, and Maria shot up it like a bat from a cave, but it petered out at the top and then took a sharp turn right and down. There was no logic to the labyrinth, it seemed designed to confuse and disorient.

We were running for our very lives. For all we'd managed to hurt De la Vega, he was still just too strong. If we were trapped in close quarters with him down here in these tightly confined spaces, we'd be buzzard feed.

Maria slid to a sudden stop, clutching tightly to keep me from flying forward and slamming into the wall in front of us. We were trapped!

Both from the pain in my ribs and the sudden rush of nausea that rose up in my belly, my knees went weak again and I collapsed. I was dazed and my breath came ragged now.

All the same, I took to thumbing my last few shells into my gun. It wasn't enough. We needed a way out. I could hear rapid footsteps tearing towards us around the corner. He was coming fast.

Maria turned, her fingers stretched out, sniffing the air, her eyes closed.

"What're you doin' gal? We need out of here! Quick!"

She turned to me, snapping her fangs, and putting a finger to her lips. I shut my yap.

She turned suddenly, began stompin' the livin' daylights out of the floor. She'd gone mad, and I couldn't blame her. What with all the excitement of late, and bein' turned into a minion of evil and all, my own complaints seemed small.

"Maria, you've got to get away. I'll hold him off so long as I can, but when I make a move, you need to git! You understand me?"

Maria ignored me, and continued just goin' to town like one o' them Mexican dancers, slamming her heels time and again on the stone.

I struggled to my feet, and steeled myself for a last stand. Hammers back, fingers tight on the triggers, it was just me and my Colts in between the love of my life and an unholy demon, hell-bent on our destruction, in a lonely dark tunnel, deep in the earth. Guess all the time I thought I done had problems, I just didn't have a clue.

De la Vega came hurtling around the corner, and I cut loose, stopping him in his tracks as he jerked and spun, heavy slugs tearing through tissue and splattering dark blood on the dark walls.

Then the floor gave way, and we fell, the three of us. My hands and feet tore at the air reflexively, like my body gone off on its own plan and figured tryin' to swim through the air was worth a shot.

My fall was suddenly arrested by a pile of rubble, and as I lay there dazed for a spell another great chunk of stone came tumbling down, crashing into my breastplate. The steel had been much abused, but it doubtless saved my life for the thirtieth time, even though I near wished it had killed me.

Strong hands yanked me free of the boulder and to my feet. I shot out a weak blow, convinced it was De la Vega, but Maria ducked under it and threw me over her shoulder again, and went tearing off down the passage. Something buried under the rubble was putting up an awful fuss, throwing boulders and great chunks of stone this way and that where they smashed to pieces against the walls.

I hung limply while Maria ran for the surface. I couldn't see my hand in front of my face now, and was fighting just to breathe. I realized in a panic I'd lost my guns!

Somehow, something about the tunnel seemed familiar, strange as that sounds. I barely knew which way was up, and couldn't have told you east from west if my life depended on it, and it well might, but perhaps it was the angle, the smell, one of those thousand things a body ignores but some part of your brain registers, and stores somewhere deep in the back of your head.

"Clay, we're almost there!" Maria confirmed, and her legs, a blur beneath me, seemed to pick up speed.

Those tell-tale eyes rose up out of the darkness in the tunnel behind us, coming up fast. Fresh fear buried the pain and I began ripping off pieces of the armor and tossing them at the vampire. It was all I had left. The armor was heavy, and I hurled it for all I was worth. De la Vega slapped most of it aside, but when I wiggled free of the sorely damaged breastplate and let it fly, it got tangled up in his legs and he went crashing down. If all the lead I'd put in him wasn't weighing him down much, I had little hopes the breastplate would do anything more than buy us a little more time. Even if we made it to the surface, he'd just go tearing into us, and then the rest of the villagers.

The angry red eyes caught up again, closing even faster. Maybe a few seconds until he caught us. Maria didn't know it, she was pushing her new body for all it was worth, but I resolved to launch myself free of her, and tackle this thing back down the tunnel just as far as I could. He'd gut me in moments, I knew, but at least it could buy her time to get away, far far away from this place. She'd sacrificed for me, and I could only hope she could understand that now it was my time to sacrifice for her.

Then of a sudden fresh air filled my lungs, and the stars blanketed the night sky above. At least I'd die on the surface, not with those cursed tunnels as my tomb.

Maria leapt, high and far, and I saw below us a line of villagers lined up in a row at the mouth of the tunnel. They held rifles. De la Vega burst forth like the devil himself out of the depths of hell, and the villagers opened fire, screaming prayers and cursing wildly in utter terror. But fire they did, and De la Vega was near torn in half from the hail of bullets. He careened back off the entrance, then clawed his way back to the mouth of the tunnel. Bullets smashed off bone and tore away chunks of blackened flesh. He turned with a terrible snarl and disappeared back down the hole like the snake he was.

Maria landed gently as a feather, and I collapsed into the dust. We were alive, for now, but De la Vega would be on his way back down his lair to set free that imprisoned army he'd been building below. Must've been at it for years. Those vampires had been locked up, starved, and they'd be utterly ravenous and vicious. Perhaps they'd be the ones that were uncontrollable, too wild and evil to even stay obedient to their master's will, but would make the perfect shock troops for the conquistador's attempt to conquer the very world. It would be wholesale slaughter.

The villager's congratulated each other, rejoicing. No doubt they thought they'd won their freedom, they'd faced down the demon what had tormented their town, their families, for so long. I pitied them. I was glad to see them resist, to fight for their freedom, but it was all pointless. If they'd begun earlier it might have saved them. Now, even a whole regiment would be torn to pieces by the coming undead army, and I didn't even have one o' them handy.

Many a time over the last day or two I'd hoped for some brilliant plan to save my skin, and just kind of had to cobble some hare-brained scheme together. But now, there was a way, one way, I might be able to stop this, and it came to me like a bolt out of the blue as I lay there, starin' up at the moon. It was crazy, something only a mad man or a desperate one could dream up. Maybe I was both. I grinned. This was the craziest thing I ever dreamed of. It had to work.

I closed my eyes, taking in the cool night air, a quick breather before the insanity I was about to wreak on Rio De Sangre. Something warm and wet nuzzled against my cheek. My eyes darted open.

My horse! The steeldust whickered in recognition. I'd no idea what had become of him, but he was back now. And he was just what I needed. That horse was one of a kind, a fact he'd proven time and again when he saved my hide from more'n one posse. He was surefooted as a mountain goat, and could run like the very wind on the prairies. Painfully, I stood and rubbed him down. He whinnied, and I whispered my plan to him. He didn't understand. He wasn't that special, but if he could speak I knew he'd be all in. He was just that kind of hoss.

I'd cheated death too many times for one day, my luck must be run clear out, but I could do what I needed to, and we'd have one hell of a last ride together. Maria stood looking at me across the street, the night wind blowing through her dark hair. The corners of her mouth turned up in a smile. She had no clue what I was about to do.

CHAPTER 19

Maria sat perched atop a section of the ruined saloon, her arms crossed. I'd just received a lesson in the sheer versatility of several Spanish cuss words, and now she just glared at me in silence. According to her, I was estupido once again, also insane, reckless, careless, arrogant, overconfident, brash, and most of all, estupido.

I didn't bother to point out she'd mentioned estupido twice, she seemed to like that word, at least as applied to yours truly. I set about the preparations, using one of the locals who spoke English better'n I did Spanish, which still wasn't sayin' much.

I sat on a wagon, rolling a smoke with the last of my tobacco, while the peasants lugged boxes of dynamite and barrels of gunpowder out of the stables, loading them onto the wagon. We lined them as best we could with straw, wet down good and proper so hopefully it wouldn't catch fire from the torches we'd attached all around the wagon. My hopes were that it might light my way and at the same time keep those foul critters back off my cargo, at least until the proper time.

A few more of the villagers set to gathering what spare rifles and weapons they could find, handing them up to me where I stowed them in handy places all around the wagon. I checked each to be sure they were loaded full, and sorted the various types of ammunition, setting bandoliers and leather pouches where I could grab them quick. If something should go wrong I wanted to be able to take as many of them with me as I could, more out of a sense of pure cussedness than a hope it would do any good.

This wagon was the very definition of hell on wheels. Loaded up full of dynamite and black powder, the rest of my armory included a double brace of old, rusty Walker Colts, brought out by an old man, neglected but still serviceable. I didn't ask where he got them. The huge horse pistols sported nine inch barrels, and weighed pretty durn close to five pounds each. I took a hammer and nails and attached a length of rope to the front of the wagon, thrusting the pistols through loops.

A few 1873 rifles were loaded full, hammer down on a cartridge in each chamber and lay ready to pump out bullets just as fast as I could use the lever. They were the cavalry model, nice and handy with 22 inch barrels. They'd hold a bit less ammo, but with four of them to burn through, I'd be lucky if I got to fire that much. A pair of single shots rounded out my arsenal, and a pouch full of copper cased .45-70 government rounds sat next to me on the buckboard. I was loaded for monster.

I missed my Colts, but I replaced them with the double barrel pistols I'd lost earlier, I was just able to stuff them down in my holsters, but they took some prying to get loose. They were my last ditch weapons. If I had need of them, it was probably irrelevant how fast they came out. Besides, that was pretty much the only way to carry them.

This was all assuming I'd make it that far. My plan, which had caused Maria such consternation, was to get into one of the wider tunnels with the wagon, and ride the wood and powder bomb on down to that great hall lined with coffins. It was the only way I could figure to get that many of them at once, and I'd no doubt De la Vega was even now settin' that undead army free. I had to make it, and get there before they made it out, or there'd be no stopping them.

The villagers were still picking weapons off the dead soldiers, bringing out ancient rifles, and building piles of logs ready to be set aflame like a burning barrier they could shoot through. They were finally ready to fight, but it would not be enough.

It had to be done. I hoped Maria could see that.

I stuffed my hat down over my ears and flicked the cigarette away. Maria had walked down the street, her senses reaching out, and somehow done found where a wide section of the tunnel lay right beneath the main street of the town. My horse stood ready in the traces. Groups of sweating, grunting men were hauling barrels of the local brew and whatever dynamite and powder wouldn't fit in the truck and were tossin' them on down every tunnel they knew of. It was time.

I turned to tip my hat one last time to my dark beauty, but she was gone. It was just as well, better for her to get over me now. I knew I'd need all the luck I could get to even make it down the twisting coils of passages below, let alone light the fuse and find my way out before the whole blew wide open. I'd been burning through favors from Lady Luck for some time now, and she must be getting tired of old Clay Wilder and his antics.

"Hey, Estupido." It was Maria, appearing out of nowhere, right behind me. That was going to get a'mighty irritating.

"Come to wish me goodbye?" I asked, trying to sound easy and light.

"No you big dumb lug, I am going with you."

Maria stood with her hands on her hips, daring me to defy her. The tiny gal looked almost comical, a cavalry sword hanging off a sash across her waist, a rifle slung across her back, her skirts torn and dirty. She was beautiful, stunning, deadly and dangerous.

"Maria..." She shushed me before I could utter another word. Just as well, since I didn't have a clue what to say, other than I didn't want her to die with me. This plan was suicidal; I was volunteering to go back into those cursed tunnels for what... the third time now? Like she said. Estupido.

"You're going to need all the help you can get. I'm not letting you do this alone. When I was down there, trapped, I knew you would come for me. I didn't want you to, but I knew you would. You came in the armor of my fairytale knight, to fight my enemies and protect me with your life. And it gave me hope. If you don't make this…insane plan work, these people will have no hope." She met my eyes, "And in a world without you, neither will I."

The words, spoken and unspoken, hung in the air between us like a cloud of cigarette smoke.

"It will be dangerous," was my last stand.

"Don't worry," she taunted, "I will protect you."

Now that tears it. I leaned over and hauled her up beside me, ignoring the screaming pain in my ribs, for once. A grin stretched across my face. I lit a stick of dynamite and handed it to her. She tossed it in front of the horse and wagon, and I had the sense for once to plug my ears.

KABOOM!

The street collapsed ahead of us, a cloud of thick smoke rising out of the gaping hole. Jagged edges of rock were barely visible, it looked like a giant fanged mouth, belching smoke.

"Light it!" I called, and a man with a torch ran forth and lit the long double fuse we'd rigged, a length of rope with just the right amount of powder rubbed in, set up for a long, slow burn. I wanted to at least know I'd a chance of making it out of there before my wagon-bomb took the place down. I had another fuse set up right by me in case something went wrong. No turning back now.

"YAAAH!" I shouted, and snapped the reigns. My horse, game as any that ever walked the earth, heaved, his steel shoes digging hard into the dirt. The wagon creaked, began to roll, and then lurched forward. Folks gathered round, shoving against the wagon to get it rolling. I couldn't tell if they just wanted to help me get a move on or if they just really wanted a torch covered wagon filled with explosives out of there as soon as possible. The wagon rumbled, the steel dust broke into a run. We plunged into the darkness.

CHAPTER 20

My heart leapt up in my throat as the wagon dropped like a stone through the hole. The wheels bounced and clattered, but the axles held and we shot down the sloped tunnel like a bullet down a barrel. I couldn't help but look back at my explosive cargo, but if the crash was gonna set it off I reckon I would have already knowed, right quick.

The tunnel was wide enough for the wagon, but barely so, and the wheels scraped the rock walls here and there throwing a shower of sparks all over the place. It was bad enough I'd lined the wagon with torches, now I had to worry about the fuse catching flame a good deal closer up than it should have been. Nothing I could do about it though, 'cept ride hell for leather down to the very heart of that evil place, and hope for one last stroke of luck.

The tunnel turned sharply, the wheels slid hard around, and the wagon slammed hard into the wall, rattling my teeth and shooting sharp knives of pain through my ribs. The cargo shifted, and the wagon went up on two wheels, careening down the steep slope. I threw myself to the other side to counter it, and Maria braced herself and kicked off hard against the wall. The other set of wheels slammed down, and I near fell off, one boot tucked under the buckboard was the only thing keeping me from falling and being crushed under the wheels. The blood rushed to my head, I had a real good view of the axle and wheel spinning. There was nothin' to grab hold of, but a small, strong hand snatched me up by the back of my shirt and back into the wagon.

The tunnel bottomed out and then rose slightly, the horse ahead running for all he was worth, not so much pulling the wagon anymore as trying to outrun it, the downhill slope was taking care of that.

The floor of the tunnel seemed to disappear, sloping sharply downward, and we screamed. The wagon was airborne for a second or two, then hurtled down, the wheels catching for a second here and there before finally settling into the grade. The tunnel narrowed, and Maria and me ducked low, the wheels brushing the rock walls. If I'd knowed it would be this tight I would have greased back my ears. The horse was pounding out a rapid staccato up ahead. Maria gripped the buckboard, white knuckled. I snapped the reins, urging the horse on, we'd need every bit of pull to get this here stagecoach to hell through this section of the tunnel.

It was no good, the wagon ground to a stop, wheels sending up showers of sparks, my horse pulling for all he was worth. I snapped the reins again and again.

"Come on hoss! Pull!" I shouted. The steeldust's great muscles strained against the load, hooves scraping against hard stone, the stallion blowing hard and trying with all it's might to get the wagon moving again. We was trapped! I cast an anxious glance toward the burning fuse.

"Clay, we've got to get moving!" Maria helpfully pointed out.

"Don't you think I know that?" I shouted back.

"We're stuck!" She exclaimed in exasperation. She was bein' real helpful. If I ever lacked a sense of the obvious, well, I knew my gal would be right there to back me up.

"Come on, you lousy mule! Pull!"

The horse whinnied back, and I'd be willing to bet there was a snide remark somewhere in there, but I didn't speak horse talk any more'n I spoke Espanol, but you could get the gist of the sarcasm if you were listening.

Somewhere a great keening noise rose up from the depths of the tunnels, and my blood ran cold. I had a guess as to what it was. De la Vega was freeing the things in the coffins, vampires from maybe centuries past, monsters he'd been preparing for this day, layin' cold and hungry and dreaming of unholy slaughter, now unleashed upon the world of man.

Maria leapt off the wagon and started pushing. The wagon scraped, steel against stone, the sound made me cringe. I snapped the reins again, and we moved forward. An inch. Maria grunted, using her unnatural strength, coupled with the steeldust's sinew and bone, and the wagon budged again.

Maria screamed with the effort, my horse lowered his head and kicked forward, again and again. Nothing happened, we'd just jammed the wagon further.

Then the floor gave way. We dropped through, the wagon crashed hard, a wheel popped clean off and flew past my face, missing my head by inches. My teeth felt like they'd been rattled clean out of my head, My horse hit the ground running, and the wagon jerked forward, skidding along the edge where the spot now missing a rear wheel sunk to the ground. The axles screeched in protest, but we were off down another steep slope. Maria clung to the back, her feet flying in the air.

I dropped the reins and launched myself across the boxes of dynamite just as the wagon skidded and slammed hard into rock, a sudden turn.

Just then, one of Maria's hands tore free, holding a chunk of wood. She hung on by one arm, the wagon goin' faster down that slope than anything I'd ever been on in my life. I stuck out an arm, and Maria grasped it with a sudden swelling of strength. I thought she'd rip my own clean off. I gritted my teeth and pulled hard, and she climbed up into the back. A sudden drop and shock and we were thrown back into the buckboard, a tangle of arms and legs. In a flash, Maria disentangled herself, suddenly sitting upright in the buckboard, grabbing the reins. It took me a bit longer, 'specially since the buckboard was buckin' about like an East Texas steer.

"Your plan is looking worse and worse every second Clay!" Maria snapped, and amid the clash and clatter of

wood and horseshoes on rock, I thought I heard another muttered "Estupido."

I grabbed wood and held on for dear life as we rocked and
slid on down the tunnel, covering what had taken me hours
before in mere minutes.

The tunnel dipped down a'sudden and then ramped up,
and we was airborne. My horse whinnied in fear as he tried
to dig in his heels but the wagon had slammed him in the
rump and we all went up in a big arc.

We shot into that wide room filled with candlelight, and
came down with a crash, the steeldust's hooves scrambling
for purchase, the wagon swinging wide, scattering torches
and boxes as it turned over. Sickly looking vampires were
crushed or knocked flying from the wagons path. Hideous
creatures turned to snarl at us. They were bent and twisted,
their hides sickly shades of green and gray. Their heads were
misshapen, oversized jaws and sharp claws. These were
De la Vega's rejects, kept imprisoned as a last resort. They
practically flowed through the doorway at the far end of
the room, staggering about, skittering sideways, skinny and
starved-looking. It was the most terrifying sight of them all.
They shrieked with hunger, and shuffled towards us.

"These ones will be weaker than all the others, we can do
this Clay!" Maria shouted, going for her Winchester.

I stood, my hands clutching at the first long gun I could
get hold of, a .45-70 single shot. Snatching up the pouch,
I drew a bead and fired, my victim's head near exploded.
Lifting the trapdoor, I fed another round in the action and
fired again. The next round tore open a creature's throat,
then the heavy slug took off the jaw of the critter behind it.
Maria opened up with the Winchester carbine, leverin' the
action like you'd pump a well, practically sprayin' bullets
with vampiric speed. I kept up the pace with the single shot
as best I could, 'til one of those blamed copper cased rounds
swelled and stuck fast in the chamber. I dropped the rifle, no
time to try and get a knife in there and work it free, and there

were others. I fetched up a Winchester and thumbed the hammer back, snapping a shot at a charging monster, crawling at me sidestep with an eerie gait. Two rounds served to drop the starved hellion in a shrieking pile, and I stomped down hard with my boot on its jaw. The shrieking stopped. These vampires were undoubtedly weaker, but what they lacked in strength they made up for in numbers.

There was no tellin' how long De la Vega had been at this. Some of the creatures wore remnants of modern clothes, looking like peasant farmers and outlaws, others wore a mere breechcloth and little bits of gold through their ears. Despite the danger, I couldn't help but shudder at the thought of bein' turned into one of these creatures, then shut up in a box for centuries, hungry for blood that'd never come. The fact that I was the only body in the room with a pulse was not lost on me, and I worked that lever with every bit of speed I could muster.

Maria aimed, fired, aimed, fired, and moved so fast she was a blur. I considered myself something of a gunhand, and vampire or no, I felt a mite undone by the little gal in the tattered dress, become hell on wheels with a long gun. I didn't know if she'd handled much in the way of shooting irons before, or if it was just her newfound powers, but she dished out death like the angel thereof.

Maria threw down her rifle and snatched up another, and went to town with it. Vampires scattered back in sudden terror, then ran into the ones pouring out of the door beyond the great stone chair. Some were so maddened they started tearing at each other, but here and there one screamed in frustration and charged, and Maria or I would bring it down in a burst of gunfire.

This couldn't last for much longer. They would charge all at once, and soon.

I let another empty gun fall from my hands. One of the stronger fiends leaped across the room, suddenly pinning me to the floor. Maria fired two more rounds through one vampire's head then took a step and smashed the butt of her Winchester into yet another's neck, sending bone and wood splinters flying.

The vampire crouched on my chest and opened its jaws wide. I grabbed a hold of another single shot by the barrel and smacked him across the face with it, then turned it and fired. The bullet went up through its throat and out the top of his head, and he disintegrated, covering me in hot cinders.

I shook off the remains, and leapt to my feet. That's when they charged, roaring as one angry beast, withered arms and legs falling all over each other as they came on like a wave of pure, misshapen evil.

I dove for the remnants of the wagon, snatching at the heavy horse pistols I'd stowed there, still attached to the buckboard. With one in each hand, I whirled and faced the oncoming wave.

As bad as the situation was, the horse pistols felt reassuring in my hands the way only eight-odd pounds of revolver can. Maria was at my side in a flash, a pair of lever guns at the ready. It was time to unleash holy hell.

CHAPTER 21

They came at a rush, and if they hadn't been so starved and weakened we would've been instantly swept away in the tide. The heavy guns soaked up much of the recoil, and I just dealt lead like a drunkard deals cards, liberally and all over the place.

The heavy slugs ripped into the crowd of oncoming monsters, sending mottled flesh flying, the screams of the damned echoed off the walls in a hellish cacophony. I tossed the empty revolvers into the crowd, and turned, my fingers wrapping around the second pair. Everything was screams and the smell of burnt powder and brimstone, ashes and gunsmoke combining to form a thick cloud. My guns barked and roared, twisted monsters toppled and writhed, turning to a puff of flying cinders before they hit the ground.

Maria fired both rifles at once, snapped them down by the lever, then back up again, and cut loose a second volley. She was a one woman death machine. Her eyes flashed with wrath and ruin, she cut loose mercilessly on the monstrous horde.

Faster than we could cut them down, the freed vampires swarmed the doorway at the far end of the room. We wouldn't be able to keep them off us much longer. Our cargo delivered, the most important thing now was to get away.

I put my last shot through a bat-like face, and dropped the heavy pistols. I ran for the fuse, ducking low to catch up another trapdoor on the way. My left hand plunged into the bag of shells, they bristled from my fist and I shot another creature through the spine, he dropped and began pulling himself towards us in swift, jerky moves.

The fuse was burning down. Might have enough time to get out, might not. We might as well try, since we were less than welcome here.

Where was De la Vega?

I lobbed shots into the crowd, flipping open the trap door, picking another round from where they jutted from my supporting hand and jamming them home, dropping the door, and repeating the process.

Clay! Watch out! Behind you!" Maria shouted over the racket she was making with her second pair of Winchesters.

Instantly, I threw myself to the ground, a sharp blade whistled over my head. I rolled, just in time to miss being cut in half as the blade reversed itself, throwing sparks as it slashed across the stone.

I leapt back, just out of reach of another stroke that sliced my shirt, it was that close. I hit the ground hard, certain any moment the flashing blade would cleave my head in two. Reflexively, my arm shot up, even if it was a useless gesture.

A loud clash of steel rang inches from my face. My eyes opened, Maria grimaced with the effort of holding back De la Vega's sword, her cavalry saber locked with De la Vega's elegant espada.

De la Vega sneered, backhanding Maria across the face. I kicked him in the shins. Maria shook off the blow and advanced, De la Vega retreated, their swords flashing with vampiric speed. De la Vega was greatly weakened from all the damage he soaked up, but he was still a trained swordsman, Maria for all her speed and newfound strength screamed in frustration as her vicious attacks were turned aside again and again. I drew my own sword, fetched up a torch and tossed it into the crowd of vampires, three of them went up in a burst of flame, the others scrambled out of the way, giving us a temporary reprieve. Those who caught fire anyway scrambled into still more, and the horde erupted in chaos and flame. It would buy us a few seconds we desperately needed. De la Vega had used those seconds too, turning the attack, and now Maria was on the retreat.

I charged, shouting. De la Vega whirled at the last second to bat away my blade, and I lost my balance as he spun away, ducking under a vicious blow from Maria's saber. I gathered up a few more torches, tossing them this way and that, and leapt atop my horse, who was wheelin' and snortin' in the traces, booting vampires clear across the room as they sought to sink their sharp fangs into his hide. That's my horse.

I clutched a handful of his mane and leaned back, slashing the tethers tying us to the wagon. The steeldust leapt forward, trampling a hapless vampire beneath his hooves, cinders and ash flying everywhere. I stuck one of the long torches through my belt to the side keeping the flames as far from me as possible.

"Clay, you've got to get out of here! You still have time!" Maria gasped, dodging a lightning thrust from De la Vega's blade.

Maria fought wildly, but fiercely, and that was the only thing keeping De la Vega from skewering her through. He ducked a blow and darted forward, his sword under Maria's guard. The blade plunged through her thigh, and she screamed. He yanked the sword free and twisted back around, shoving it this time through her shoulder. I ducked to one side, my leg hooked around the horse, my fingers buried in its mane. I flung my sword. I watched in horror as De la Vega spun again, slashing his sword across Maria's throat.

The blood poured out in a heavy torrent, like a river when a dam breaks. It poured down her dress. She dropped the saber. My world shattered. The saber clattered to the floor. She started to fall.

My sword flew through the air like a dart. Maria sank to her knees. De la Vega, poised for the final blow, staggered back a step as my blade stabbed deep, burying the point through his shoulder.

Shouting wordlessly, I leaned out, my fist smashed into

De la Vega's face. One of his fangs went flying. Bolt's of lightning shot up my arm, but then it was numb and I tucked my elbow around Maria's waist and heaved, pulling her up over my lap onto the horse.

I ducked low under the doorway, and we sped off up the tunnel. A wild, inhuman chorus of damned souls lifted up their ragged voices behind us, but one was louder than them all. De la Vega.

CHAPTER 22

I slapped the reins right and left, but the horse needed no encouragement. Bent low over Maria, I felt her wound with my fingers, barely able to see, the torch flickering dimly behind me.

Her wound was wide open, still leaking blood all down the sides and flanks of my horse, covering my trousers.

No! She could not die! I would not allow that to happen. My sword gone, I searched for anything on my person sharp enough to cut open a vein. I had none. The skin around Maria's eyes shrunk up, she was losing the last of her blood. She would die, a lasting death this time.

Without further thought, I grabbed her by the hair, ripping her head back. Her mouth fell open, and I jammed my wrist against her teeth, the fangs puncturing deep into my arm.

Maria's eyes shot open. They were blank, lifeless. Her face twisted horribly and she bit down hard, I feared she would crush my arm. She drank greedily, sucking the blood from my veins. She was utterly focused, her eyes rolled back in her head as she tasted her first draught of human blood. I felt suddenly lightheaded, swaying on the horse. She would drain me dry without meaning to. The wound on her throat closed miraculously, and the pressure on my veins grew stronger as she drained the blood right from my arm.

I hated myself for it, but I drew one of my double barrels and cracked it across her forehead. She went on drinking. I did it again, and she let go, looking up at me suddenly, a flash of recognition, then her eyes closed and she faded back into unconsciousness. Blazes!

I hoped she'd spring back to life, and I could convince

her to flee with her great speed out of this place, I could hold off the coming waves long enough for her to get clear before this whole place went up in the blast. She was limp as a rag doll, but she'd live if I could find a way to get her out of here before the vampires caught up to us. If her bite would turn me into a vampire I had no way of knowing. If she hadn't lost her soul due to the sacrifice she made for me, maybe I wouldn't either. I didn't figure I'd have the time left to actually change into anything anyway, like as not we'd be ripped to pieces shortly.

My horse put his head down, and ran like the demons of hell were chasin' after him, probably 'cause they were. I risked a look over my shoulder, red eyes coming up fast, eyes glowing brighter in the torchlight.

"Come on you mule, we're ridin' for real, this time!" I shouted. That horse had saved my worthless hide from more than one posse what carried an extra length of rope, and if I had all the luck in the world he'd do it one last time.

The horse blowed, picking up speed even though he was carrying two bodies uphill, and that's no small trick. His steel shoes dug sharply into the stone flooring, beating out a clippety-clop so fast it sounded like a Gatling gun. It wasn't enough.

The vampires, weak and starved, were still gaining. Any normal horse would've run his'self to death by now. And De la Vega was back there somewhere's, I knew.

I leaned back, drew one of the doubles, and fired into the pursuers. A scream, a puff of smoke and embers, and a few cries were all I gained for my efforts. I fired again, breaking open the action to replace the shells, which is no small feat as fast as that horse was running. The vampire's cries of hunger rang up the tunnel. I cut loose with another double charge of buckshot, and turned to reload.

The dim light of the torch showed a barrel rolling down the tunnel. The peasants were still at it up there, rolling barrels of the local brew down the passages. I didn't dream they'd have so much, but it could be that most desperados were just not desperate enough to drink it. My horse hurdled the barrel, and it crashed behind us into the onrushing horde.

We hurtled another barrel, then dodged around another that had lodged at a fork in the tunnel. The steeldust's breathing was ragged, labored. But up and up he went, trading years for minutes to get me and Maria to safety. For his sake, I hoped we'd make it.

The vampire tide caught up to us, the creatures hurtled up the passageway to tear at the steeldust's flanks. Two of them caught hold of his legs, and his hooves lost purchase, skittering along a patch of smooth stone.

The horse faltered, went slamming to the ground, sliding on his belly as Maria and I were catapulted up and off, sent bouncing and tumbling along the tunnel. My rear would be sore as hell in the morning, if by some stroke of mercy I saw it. It didn't look that way, as the vampires hurdled the horse, swarmed over him, and came rushing on. I lay on my side, drew the doubles, and let them have all four shots. A cloud of choking brimstone and embers filled the tight passage, I could scarce breathe. I set to reloading, only half done when I saw something barreling through the smoke towards me.

I aimed the one gun I'd reloaded, but the steeldust leapt from the cloud of ash, neighing so loud it echoed over the cries of the vampires. He launched a mighty kick that drove back the crowd, one vamp caught it in the face and exploded in a fizzle of ash and cinders, his head stove in.

My horse whirled and bucked, lashing out with his hooves, holding back the tide. He rammed a shoulder into another vampire crushing him flat against the wall. That horse turned an eye towards me, snorted, and went a buckin' into the crowd like a wild mustang the wrong feller done picked to ride at the rodeo, and I understood. There wasn't and never would be another like him.

Straining, I picked up Maria in my arms, and took off. My insides felt like they were stabbing me to death, and my left hand couldn't quite close all the way. I was weak from blood loss and badly battered, but I manned up and put one foot in front of the other just as fast as I could.

My muscles bunched and strained, my lungs gasped for air, more air, painful as it was to breathe. Maria hung limp in my arms, and nothin's heavier than dead weight. I'd hoped she'd recover faster, she was supposed to be stronger than the others, made when De la Vega had recovered the strength he'd been centuries regaining, and so she should be able to survive a good deal more than his weaker "children". She still hung over my shoulder like a sack of flour, and there I was again, back to carryin' folks all over creation.

I didn't know how much further we had to go, but hoped it wasn't far. Each step felt like it was numbered. The steeldust had spirit in spades, but he couldn't hold them off forever.

My steps grew shorter and shorter, my legs burned with the effort, my shoulders strained to hold Maria up.

Another barrel came tumbling down, I barely sidestepped, the rim of it clipped my knee, and down I went in a heap. Gasping, I struggled to my feet, turned and grabbed Maria under her shoulders, began dragging her backwards, up, up, ever upward.

I twisted a hand into the fabric of her dress, dug my torch out of my belt, and kept pumping my legs. Not much further now, I told myself. And it was true. Either we'd find the surface, or the vampires would catch up to us, or the wagon would go off any second and bury us all beneath a pile of rubble. Any which way the cards played out, there wasn't much longer.

Two twisted creatures came running up out of the cloud below, closing fast. I readied myself for a last stand. Before they could reach me, another black figure shot up the tunnel and into the torchlight. De la Vega. He batted the others out of the way like flies; they fizzled and burst apart as their skulls were smashed against the rock walls.

I swung the torch, but he caught my hand in his and slammed his other one into my chest. I hit the ground, hard. The vampire tossed the torch back down the tunnel, seething with anger. I stood again, reaching for the hilt of the sword still buried in his chest. He hadn't even bothered to remove it, so intent was he on chasing me down. He wanted me dead almost as bad as I wanted him in an ashtray. De la Vega knocked my grasping fingers aside and backhanded me hard. I flew aside, my arm getting in between my head and the wall. The bone cracked audibly, but it saved my skull from being crushed.

My legs buckled, and I sank to my knees. De la Vega was all over me like flies on a carcass, and he snatched me up in the air. That would have been a great time for Maria to come to. Instead, I was slammed down again, my ribs made a sound I can't even describe, the wind knocked clean from me.

De la Vega put his foot on my chest, gloating. His laugh was cruel and evil, echoing off the walls. Below in the tunnel, I could hear a rising clamor. My horse had fallen. I also heard something tumbling down from above. Another barrel. I threw my head back to look, while De la Vega shouted in exultation and triumph. My chest burned, but I grabbed hold of his foot and twisted, rolling to my right. The barrel came hurtling down, bouncing and rolling, and took my nemesis out at the knees. I leapt up, grabbing for the sword he'd dropped. A sharp blow rattled my jaw from out of nowhere.

The monster snatched the sword back, kicking the barrel aside. He stuck it in my shoulder, twisted. I screamed. He laughed.

"Now, Wilder, for the very last time, do you have any final words?" He taunted.

"Yeah…" I managed, sucking in a breath, the sword pinning me to the floor, my right arm numb. I flexed my fingers. I could feel the bones grinding sharp edges against each other.

The conquistador cocked an ear.

"You talk too much."

My left hand flashed down, drawing as fast as ever I had. The twin barrels roared, De la Vega's sword fell from lifeless fingers as his blackened arm hung by a mere thread of skin. It broke, and the arm hit the ground. I kicked out, sending the vampire reeling backwards.

A volcanic rage clouded out my pain as I struggled heavily to my feet. De la Vega clutched his shoulder, and wailed piteously.

I grinned savagely at De la Vega through the blood and the grime. I waded into him with both fists, a sudden strength surging through my arms. I slugged him with my left, and it didn't hurt. I followed up with a cross, that spun him around straight into my looping left hook. He grabbed me by the throat with his remaining arm. He squeezed, but I tightened my neck, he didn't have the strength left to crush me. My face tight, I showed him my teeth. He snarled, and I bulled forward, my hands finding the hilt of the sword still stuck through him, and I drove him into the barrel, the sharp point stabbing deep into the wood. Grunting, I summoned every last bit of my strength, and put my shoulder into it, bending that steel around, wrapping it flush with the barrel, fixing him fast to the wood. There was fear in his eyes.

Panting, I dug out the last double, and fired a load of shot into the wood. Tequila ran down the sides, splattering on the floor of the tunnel.

I looked in his eyes, and fired the last shell right next to the flowing liquor. The barrel burst into flame, and De la Vega's eyes were wild. He struggled to reach across with his remaining arm and free himself. His hand slipped wildly on the blade, dark blood dripping on the floor.

"Give the Devil my regards," I snarled, and put my heel against the barrel. I launched a kick that would have made the steeldust proud, and he screamed, rolling over and over with the barrel, now a flaming projectile bouncing and tumbling into the darkness below.

A swarm of vampires broke free of the smoke and came rushing up, met by the flames, practically exploding in a shower of embers. De la Vega's screams echoed up at me for a long, long time.

The ground shook of a sudden, and I lost my footing. I hurt again.

A great loud thunderclap washed over me, followed by a wave of tumbling dust, smoke, and debris.

Rock shards stung my face and arms, I closed my mouth and scrambled, my hands finding Maria, I gathered her up in my arms and took off at a run, using the last of my strength. A chunk of rock tore free of the ceiling and crashed in front of us. I lowered my head and pumped my legs, driving forward. Great tumbling echoes vibrated through the tunnels as they collapsed below us. Chunks of stone rained down on my head and shoulders, I carried Maria low and close to shield her from the assault. All was blackness; there was no air to breathe.

I drove on, deafened by the yawning of the quaking rock below.

We burst forth into the air, a cloud of smoke and ash erupting behind us, and I tumbled to my knees, gasping.

Maria came to, suddenly screaming.

A faint pink glow lit the purple sky. The Dawn!

The sun broke the horizon in the hills to the east, and Maria started to smoulder. Her piercing cry rang out in the hills, sending the assembled villagers to their knees, clapping work hardened hands over their ears. I grabbed a man by the belt and yanked him off his horse, undoing the buckle of his saddle with one swift move. The saddle freed, I grabbed hold of the blanket underneath and ran for the writhing, smoking figure that was Maria.

I dove over her with the blanket, just as she burst into flames.

Chapter 23

I stood leaning on a shovel at the edge of the canyon, looking down over the waterfall below. I built a smoke. It was near evening, the sun was sinking into the hills to the west.

I sighed, struck a match, and took a puff. There's nothing like digging a grave for the one you love. It didn't matter that I'd barely known Maria more than a few days. She'd be the love of my life always, no matter what. In the chaos and danger of those terrible hours, something had connected between us. Something I didn't have any hope of finding again. Most folks never had it happen to them at all, so I figured, no matter what, I was ahead.

I'd been digging all day. My injuries had made it near impossible, and I should've dug it deeper, but I didn't have the strength and I had insisted I would do it myself. While I dug, long rolling tears wet my cheeks now and again, and it wasn't from the pain in my left hand or my cracked ribs. Breathing was hard, but some old gal had done a right good job of wrapping the bandages, and it only hurt when I inhaled or exhaled.

My cigarette burned down, I looked at the falling water but all I saw was her face. The villagers had laid her out proper in her mother's wedding dress. It was found in her closet when they'd looked for something suitable. Everyone was surprised to see it, since her mother had never married and was as poor as the soil in Rio de Sangre. Folks were speculating about what secret hope her mother had to save such an expensive thing and never once get to wear it. The way Maria looked in it just before they nailed the lid shut would haunt me forever.

I stared at the twin wounds on my left wrist. They'd scabbed over, and I hadn't started to smoke or smoulder, not even once, though I'd spent the day in the sun. Guess I hadn't lost enough blood, or even the devil didn't want my soul.

Even though she'd turned into a vampire, she hadn't become like them. She didn't allow herself to be changed out of a desire for power, or fear, or abandonment of faith, she did it for me. I could only guess her sacrifice had meant she had kept her immortal soul intact. If Miguel was still here I could ask him, but I knew little of such things. I was just a battered and bloody outlaw, fillin' in a grave, not a ponderer of the higher mysteries.

True, I was covered in dust, grime and ash, but my soul felt clean. For the first time since…a long time. Could make a feller think of a lot of things. Righteousness, atonement and such, crazy ideas like that. Whether that pile of gold under the stables was better off in the hands of one scruffy outlaw or if it could help a town full of poor folks. Best not to make such decisions too hastily, right? I had a lot to chew over, and a lifetime to do it.

I stubbed out the smoke and watched the sun go down. It cast long shadows over the cactus trees and rocks.

My gaze wandered over to the pile of fresh dug dirt where Maria lay. All I had time to do was tie a pair of sticks together to make a plain wood cross. I'd have to see about a headstone, but it just seemed right to make sure something was there to mark the sight. I knowed a passel of men who'd be glad to have had it, lying in unmarked graves or no graves at all, their bones bleached by the sun or picked at by coyotes.

The sun disappeared behind the hills. I rolled another smoke. Out of habit I checked my guns, a new pair of Colt Thunderer's in .41 colt. The villagers had presented me with them as a way of sayin' thank you, and I didn't ask where they come from. They were double action, meaning I could fire them as fast as I could pull the trigger, somethin' I'd come to appreciate of late.

The dirt on the grave seemed to sort of cave in on itself, a white gloved hand broke the surface.

Maria burst up in the air, throwing a shower of dirt in every direction. Somehow, she was clean as a whistle.

Maria landed smoothly, gliding towards me. Her fangs glinted in the last traces of light. She was glowing, her skin perfect and pale, just a hint of her former tan. She was beautiful. I could only guess that being the last child of De la Vega, she was also the strongest. He'd given her a lot of his blood, which must've been what allowed her to survive nearly being burnt to a crisp. I'd gotten that blanket on her just in time.

"Gonna' be a heck of a job, getting' you in and outta there every night." I said casually, taking a drag.

She zipped right up to me; one second she was a few feet away, the next she was smack dab in my face, holding my cigarette between two dainty fingers.

She flicked it away. "No fire." Her nose wrinkled.

"Oh yeah, sorry 'bout that," I drawled.

I put my arms around her.

"Shame about your brother. I'd say he went happy, but still, if'n we had a padre here, I'd ask you to marry me."

She smiled.

"I am all dressed for the occasion. But you're supposed to court me first. Aren't you going to offer to buy a lady a drink or dinner or something like that?" she said coyly.

"Just so long as it's not tequila."

I gathered her up in my arms, my mouth met hers. She melted against me, and I knew then and there that she was mine and I was hers, forever. Dang! Those fangs were sharp!

"Felices para Siempre..." Maria breathed when we came up for air.

"What's that again?" I was puzzled. The phrase was familiar, but my brain basket had been cracked around some, and I'd misplaced a good deal of blood. Between that and her kisses, I was a little lightheaded.

"Don't you remember? That's the next part. Where there are monsters, there are heroes, and my knight in armor came for me after all. That armor wasn't so shiny, the horse wasn't white, but the knight inside is what really mattered. And now we live felices para siempre. Happily ever after."

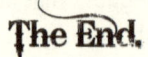

The End.

THE SAGA CONTINUES...

"Blood on the Mississippi"

When Maria and Clay leave Rio De Sangre one jump ahead of a deadly order of holy warriors, they must strike east to buy each day anew by their wits and the strength of their bond.

Their honeymoon is spent on the dodge, Clay gambles the riverboats by day to finance their headlong flight up and down the Mississippi, Maria stalks the wilderness and desolate places by night, trying to stave off her growing thirst for blood. Having little time to worry about the inevitable conclusion of a marriage between a mortal and immortal, the newlyweds can only hope to stay one step ahead of the order of Saint Michael, and their deadliest enemy yet, one who claims to be the archangel himself.

But romish assassins aren't the only thing stalking them through the night. Clay and Maria find themselves with a mysterious invitation to the most exclusive card game in the world. The stakes are a chance to win back their lives, regain their humanity, and rid themselves from the curse of the vampire. Clay will need to use every trick he's ever learned in a smoky saloon or on the hoot-owl trail to take the pot, and going bust is not an option. This time, the stakes are higher than ever, they soon discover they aren't playing for money. They are playing for their very souls, and the devil plays for keeps.

Colin Webster is a former U.S. Marine with plenty of experience in life or death situations and combat with firearms. He is intimately familiar with the weapons and armaments of the late 1800s. Colin has published biographical articles for starting strength. He has self published a western titled *Blood and Silver*. Colin lives in New Bern, North Carolina, where he works as an independent security consultant.